C000193506

the actual whole of music

the actual whole of music

haydn middleton

propolis

First published in 2021
by Propolis Books

The Book Hive,
53 London Street,
Norwich, NR2 1HL

All rights reserved
© Haydn Middleton 2021

Cover by Niki Medlik at studio medlikova
with thanks to Kendrick Mills/Unsplash

The right of Haydn Middleton to be identified
as the author of this work has been asserted
by him in accordance with the Copyright,
Designs and Patents Act, 1988

A CIP record for this book
is available from the British Library
ISBN 9780992946098

Designed and typeset by benstudios.co.uk

Printed and bound by TJ Books Limited,
Padstow, Cornwall

www.propolisbooks.co.uk

To those for ever in my heart

1

i

Back in the gramophone era you lowered a needle on to a spinning vinyl disc, and the room came alive with music.

You could say this era of our own dawned in much the same way. A needle dropped from nowhere on to an already revolving record, then the darkness thinned a little, we looked around and found ourselves at sea. Just us. A small youthful convoy, faced by a chain of mostly uninhabited islands stretching out to the west.

We never knew where we were in that earliest archipelago. No maps, no route, no plan. Nor did we think we had ever met before, so we could only guess at why we'd been singled out, and for how long we might be expected to stick together.

A few of us may well have wondered if our task was to couple up and repopulate this slowly waking world. As a cohort we didn't appear too well-equipped to take on many other responsibilities. It seemed to me even at the outset that each of us could have been anyone – anyone or no one.

The seas remained calm, as smooth at times as the sheared-off shards of land they lapped between, and island by island we searched one another's faces for signs of what we might conceivably have in common.

But when finally we felt confident enough to speak, we seldom if ever discussed the long night we'd just endured. Even when some of us experienced episodes that may have been collateral stress disorders, still almost nothing would be said, nothing shared.

The curtain had gone down on one world and risen on another. Bemused, we'd look out on endless land- and sea-scapes which held neither memories nor meaning for us.

Still more unnervingly at first, the further we journeyed under these new skies, the less we appeared to remember of all we had lived through under the old. But wherever we'd been shut away separately before, from the moment of our release our clear unspoken agreement was that there should be no going back.

The first island survivors we saw were still not attuned to the light. None of them ever came close enough to talk to us, and further down the line we deduced from one of their many reported names for us – The Choir – that to begin with they'd had limited communication among themselves as well.

But we would also find out in due course that, unlike us, they'd agreed on a name for the monumental rupture beforehand. The blackout, they called it. And for all our own rich assortment of skin colours, we in the cohort found ourselves comfortable using this term too, covering as it did not only the unnaturally extended night but also the vagueness (at that stage still possibly temporary) in our recall of its shape and nature.

Perhaps there was no language for everything that had happened. In its immediate aftermath, there seemed barely to be a language for emotions. Across the board, it was as if all trust in words had ended.

The darkness gave way to laughter. That would be one way of describing this next phase, but the process was a slow one.

For the longest time all we knew by day was first light, as if a single drizzly autumnal morning was forever breaking.

A lingering dimness clung to the underside of the air, forming a dank membrane between ourselves and full sunlight, as though light itself would only drizzle, refusing to gather into anything approaching a beam, so we saw everything, including one another, through a frosted pearly veil.

This must have added to our sense of very gradually coming awake; even, at times, of walking in our sleep.

Twenty-six small longboats made up our fleet; "pinnaces" as some of the girls who formed half our initial complement of ninety decided they should be called.

As with so much else in this opening period, the vessels seemed both new and yet full of echoes: wickerwork frames with sewn tanned hides stretched over; at the stern of each was a large steering oar, then benches for nine rowers, although few of them ever seated anything like that number, while amidships stood a mast fitted with a three-cornered sail of soft pale leather which mainly went unused.

As often as not, we would just put up our oars and allow what gentle currents there were to take us on.

We never stayed anywhere long – a night or a day in each new place – and all our arrivals were both expected and catered for.

On most of the islands our dedicated residential blocks could be found at once, either on the coast or else just a short walk inland. Each was fitted out to exactly the same specification: part pillbox, part hostel, part large sports dressing room giving on to an adjoining shower area.

In some of the open-plan dressing rooms there would be a token row of changing cubicles for privacy, and the dorms were always rigorously segregated. Otherwise we young men had to pitch in together with the young women – an arrangement, we later learned, that stirred considerably more interest outside our group than within it.

All of us had our own lockers, their numbers matching those we found inked on to tags inside our coats; and sometimes, as well as provisions and medications (both prescribed and recreational), books for overnight reading came from these lockers, along with fresh issues of clothing to withstand the fine, persistent rain.

Even when we stayed over at requisitioned summer houses like the one which would later be known as Voormann Park Museum, the facilities would be similar: these same shadowy dressing rooms with their faint high tang of menthol and eucalyptus.

The first thin scatter of islanders we saw were either much older or much younger than ourselves. In other ways they seemed identical to our own group, and of much the same ethnic mix, as remained the case through all our travels.

A few of the adults wore ragged white armbands, perhaps to indicate surrender. Some also had deeply-stained burlap bindings at their wrists; around the necks of others still were strung pouches that may have held cyanide capsules.

Although these people stayed well away from our blocks, whenever we left out for them what little food we could spare in its original vacuum packaging, it would always be gone by the morning. Even when we took it on ourselves to pay respects at their carefully-tended burial grounds, we'd constantly be aware of them observing us from a safe distance.

There was no opportunity to tell them that we, too, were feeling our way forward. At this point we were hardly even speaking to one another. The whole world seemed to be pausing for breath: it's no exaggeration to say that the way we talked was closer to swapping lines from songs or poems than holding a conversation. Young and diffident as we were, we'd often trade wry catchphrases too, their context or meaning long since lost to us, although some of them did not seem entirely empty.

'No matches, no sharp objects!' one of us might murmur as we watched a group of infants play in the wreckage of an old car; another might then say, 'Our parents had to let us go' or 'Don't expect miracles', which would possibly trigger a smile.

There were also one or two coinages that felt newer – terser quips like 'We used to know that', 'It all adds up', and the one we bandied about most freely of all: 'So this is us!'

But we were new to the islanders; even when at successive settlements they started to heavily outnumber us, they'd remain out of range whilst watching our every move with a look of both panic and pity.

After all the trials of their blackout, its finer points perhaps still vivid in their minds, many may have seen in us a warning shot of challenges still to come. But our sudden appearance out of nowhere could also have been read as a turning of the tide – for them, for us all – and this may have helped give our little island-hopping fleet whatever chance it had.

Then, again and again, we would be back out on the water, manoeuvring our westward way to the next link in the island chain, the books back in their lockers, coat sleeve brushing coat sleeve whether carelessly or by design.

These coats we wore so tightly wrapped around ourselves came in various forms: waxed waterproof jackets, gabardines, fake furs and scarves for the most part; an ex-serviceman's black double-breasted greatcoat in my own case.

Uncorrupted images from Voormann Park's archive would one day show college students from pre-blackout times similarly dressed, although few of us would ever have been at home in any seat of learning: not all our boys learned to read, some barely mastered speech. So whenever we were in transit, it seemed natural for a core group of our girls to take a kind of lead.

These girls, like us boys, had long hair mostly, uncomplicated styles spilling down over their shoulders. Their make-up and piercings were more discreet than the loud fluorescent watch-straps and outsized hooped earrings they seemed to take it in turns to wear. They'd give an impression that they had been on the journey before, though not in so many words, and not necessarily taking this particular route.

Instead they gave subtle signs that the logic of our progress might not be a total surprise, for example in the way they referred with confidence to our longboats as pinnaces; more specifically, "ship's pinnaces", suggesting an earlier transfer from larger craft before we set off on our winding path through all the fragments.

These things could have been picked up from the locker books which they made more of a show than us boys of reading; books they sometimes scribbled their own names in, not on the flyleaf but more collaboratively next to that of the author on the title page.

Some of them also made entries in a form of log which I'll be coming back to, but again they went about this work longhand, using pens and notebooks.

There was no question back then of computers, or screens, of accessing information via sources like that. There was scarcely any power at all, electrical or otherwise, except for the activity inside our minds, plus the probably inevitable sexual charge we eventually began to generate and store up among ourselves.

What's undeniable is that this particular handful of girls had an instinct for the next approaching landfall, a sixth sense which told them a new island was about to hove into view.

We would watch one rise to her feet in the boat, dreamy-eyed and slinky, as if she'd been hooked on a thread from a shore still invisible to the rest of us.

She'd shimmer then where she stood, maybe just a single slow twitch of the hips inside her coat, the laziest of winks with the length of her body, and when she sat down again, suppressing a smile, we would turn on our rowing benches and invariably we'd soon see something new on the horizon.

If you asked how long this went on I would have to say lifetimes, inasmuch as any of us then knew what a lifetime was. (When we set out, our youngest were still not shaving, while those of us with beards seemed to get no older, and certainly no wiser.)

Little back then could be measured or classified in the ways used later. For all that everything appeared to be happening in rising light, there must have been as many nights as marching mornings, phases of relative stillness. But these we could only recall in fond fragments, through bonfire-lit hazes fuelled by dope and booze – because as we went along, we continued to forget. We'd all known so much darkness before: maybe this worked now as a check on more recent memories, largely filtering out newer times without light.

And within that pearly ether, time really did seem to move differently, more loosely – most of the ruined structures we saw looked like the result of centuries of decay rather than recently-inflicted damage – but we knew of no faster route to the future.

We also had no way of telling if we were leading these charmed lives of ours on borrowed time. So although we must often have looked hopelessly callow to the more life-hardened islanders, with all due respect to them we never ourselves spoke of "the" blackout, as if there mightn't be another. Maybe in our hearts we never stopped feeling it all might end any day. Instead it just kept starting.

But headway was still being made. The gramophone disc continued to spin, we followed its spiral path.

At the best times our progress felt as lucid as one thought leading to another. In looking always forward, we could let more unsettling aspects of the past drift like wreckage on the seas in our wake, hoping it might eventually sink from view.

Meanwhile as a collective, we grew closer.

Yes, there were some small frictions. Squabbles, stand-offs. In the dimly-remembered nights there would be screams, while for long periods some of us refused to travel in the same boats as certain others. But we had formed bonds of love – initially of the type found within an extended group of siblings or cousins – and while we couldn't know whether or not this was all part of some grand providential design, with every spent day we felt richer.

That was ultimately what gave our travelling its sense of release. Release more than escape, because if ever we'd felt we were on the run from anyone or anything, this no longer seemed to be so.

Having learned during our time together to count our blessings, for us it was only ever "to". Toward.

A place had to be awaiting us – one we'd know as home.

ii

We had been approaching the final island in this phase for so long, it's possible we soaked up some of its atmosphere even before setting foot on its shingle.

Zhiyin, a honey-skinned girl in a thin cotton smock, stood up in her boat to give us notice. One serpentine sway and there it was: a sudden granite sea-tooth capped by scrubby heath, an island of visibly older formation than any we'd so far visited.

High above our disembarkation point an immense figure had weathered naturally into the slope. An ageing face in profile with one dark socket for an eye, and below it – standing as if to attention – a clearly-defined rock body.

We didn't all wear coats that morning: for a few of us it was shirtsleeves, sandals, shorts. With everyone in coats we were still, you might say, on the march. But here in this warmer, slightly drier environment, with the porcelain-white sky making an echo chamber for the basking seals' strange fraught wails, already it seemed unlike any of our more regular stopovers.

As we hiked up the cliff steps then ambled around the coastal path, our tread seemed lighter. There was no sign of a residential block nor any kind of settlement, but as we made for the interior the island itself felt alive. Its surface could have been rising and falling to the rhythms of shallow sleep. Sleep, or the first stirrings of some unimaginable music.

This downland had an ambience all its own: rolling chalk hills of the kind you'd expect to see in a more landlocked space.

When we entered the deepest of the dry valleys from the north, the well-grassed bank facing us was the steeper of the two, with a wide flat-topped knoll offering a convenient natural platform for viewing its gentle folds in either direction.

The knoll was large enough for us all to step up on to it.

It's doubtful whether any of us had spoken since leaving the shoreline. The stillness of the place beat in our ears. Shoulder to shoulder we stood, rank on rank, all eyes trained on the section of the incline straight ahead.

Before we felt any new warmth on our necks, the first thing we saw were silver coins of light dappling the steep wall of grass. Soon these resolved into a single pale impression.

There, against the tussocks, lay a huge three-cornered shape like one of our boats' lateen sails which we so seldom put to use – and briefly it seemed to ripple, a sheet dimpled by wind.

On stilling itself, however, it took on a different, three-dimensional appearance, as if formed by cutting out a great triangular wedge of turf to show the chalk underneath.

We grasped that a pioneering shaft of sunlight must at last have pierced the mother-of-pearl membrane. But this did not entirely explain what we saw, because all around the triangle the rest of the slope appeared to have receded like a darker tide of earth.

Then the light-form tilted, as if to balance on just one of its points.

Our pulses raced at what we saw. For a moment, all the previously-hidden light in the heavens seemed to pass through a lens to create a shape resembling the space within a harp's frame where the strings stretch across. Then before our eyes the shape's fluid line changed again to become that of a stylized human heart, one which – as even the finest rain ceased – appeared to be beating.

We knew what to do.

Without a glance behind or above, we began to funnel down from the knoll and climb up to where the heart continued to pulse. No thread that ever hooked one of our girls out at sea could have drawn us up more steadily.

Our front line hesitated at its perimeter to allow those behind to fan out, so that everyone was then in a position to enter at much the same time.

It felt like stepping into a sanctuary. There was room inside for every one of us to stretch out flat on the ground, at all angles, while staying in at least marginal contact with those who were the nearest.

Only then, through narrowed eyes, did we look upwards.

There was, of course, nothing to see.

The dazzle was too great. But as the heat seared down, a satisfied murmur passed among our whole company, as if it was us who had been responsible for luring the sun through the membrane and back into place.

But whether we'd been laying down or following a trail, this looked like an exit, or possibly even an entrance. Dovetailed inside the heart made of light, we waited to find out which.

The heat on our faces grew fiercer. The mellow vibrations cut out, but if the celestial gramophone needle had momentarily been lifted from the record, then in a powerful sensory rush I felt myself rising with it, up out of the group, out of myself.

Just what had led us to this moment can be endlessly debated; so too can what happened afterwards, or didn't. The very notion of "a moment" could be argued over, as could that of only one path ever leading between a pair of them. The light was shaking everything free, filling the gaps in what we thought we knew.

I saw us as if from above, a display of glass chips in a tray, where all our own colours had new life; yet all that seemed to matter was the pattern. A window had opened, a door, one we could go through together or not at all.

"So this could be us," I might've modified our catchphrase to say, had I not been so transfixed: in step, in concert, in a new kind of love, so closely woven into one another's lives that in the end we would speak direct from heart to heart. One world had been blasted apart but here was its reverse, an elegant heart of light corralling our cohort ever closer, just us – at least in the first instance – until one of us might stretch and the rest feel the tingle in our fingertips.

It seemed this truly could make sense: each of us no more than a stripe on the tiger's flank, barely individual enough to have strictly personal thoughts or drives. It maybe explained why our more singular histories had already been wiped from our minds. And there was such beauty in the prospect of what might be about to take their place that tears rose to my eyes.

But this was also the unknown, so it was chilling.

And then a new sound distracted me.

I was so swept up that at first I took it to be birds, the yatter of faraway magpies, but in fact it was coming from us, rustling in from our outer fringes then back out again: giggles.

Giggles that fast became snorts. Swirls then of belly laughter, a noise so unfamiliar it now had the power to alarm.

It shocked me into noticing I had lost contact with everyone else, and in rocking myself upright I blinked.

There was no distinct heart any more. Its fresh clear light lay diffused across the entire seen landscape, and we were all back inside the borders of ourselves.

Wiping my eyes on the back of my hand, it was impossible for me not to join in with the general merriment – out of sheer relief at the sun's full return after so long, or else at our own outlandish good fortune.

But people can laugh for many reasons, and while I laughed I watched, and I saw what the islanders may have shrunk from seeing in me and my peers all along: such vulnerability, helpless immaturity, a band of untested nomads, eyes glazed with reefer, kicking our legs in the air like capsized woodlice, some of us already half out of our flimsy clothing and starting to cavort.

This, too, was us. Not so indistinguishable from those who didn't travel, all those non-itinerants we had assumed to be casualties of whatever had gone before. And as I went on laughing I had to wonder why – with any kind of mainland still no more than a rumour – we had always been so free among ourselves with the term "islanders". What then did that make us?

This was long before we heard any island tales that our group had come, quite literally, from nowhere – transposed from a place which did not yet exist.

There would be so many legends; that we were insane or divine, penal transportees or deposed royalty. Even inside our own cohort the girl I would come to love best – my poor dear Lani – put it out that we had died and entered an afterworld.

I can't say how seriously such talk was ever meant to be taken. And what I'm about to suggest must not detract from all the wonders we were still to witness, both inside the cohort and out, before this cycle of events was complete. But while I will always suspect our exposure to the heart of light was a turning point in our travels, it may also have marked a turning away.

It's a large and potentially ludicrous thing to ask (and until writing this I've never dared broach it with anyone), but if we'd held our nerve for just a little longer on that cusp of an afternoon, and not laughed quite so soon, then instead of forging on under the new light into an arguably chequered future, might there have been a different kind of a homecoming, and not just for ourselves?

2

iii

Whether or not we now entered a new archipelago, during the next lengthy phase of our expedition the islands we stopped at had much the same natural appearance as before.

The seas too were no less placid.

It's probably fairer to describe what we passed into as a new "field", where our interactions with certain islanders, and more especially with one another, went through a dramatic alteration.

Forgive me if some of what I cover next comes out of sequence. I've never had the strongest sense of time, and before this account, the only writing ever required of me took the form of random impressions, with no need to try to separate out causes from effects. I'd hoped to quickly string together here a narrative of specific events, like features you might see from a moving boat (and there will be some of these) but so much unfolded in terms of a longer-term process, of transition.

It may nonetheless be inaccurate to see in each new development a pointer towards this phase's sudden, decisive ending. And it's hard to see all the individuals in our group as anything other than unfinished articles, still in an almost chrysalid state.

As such, island by island, we were more absorbed in trying to work out what we ourselves might become than in paying proper attention to what we were moving through – a world at this new dawn of time in which the patterns of the days and seasons were so rapidly reconfiguring.

Quite soon it became clear that the further we travelled, the more intact by and large that world's built environment would look. Many of the smaller settlements showed fewer signs of a previous shattering, and at least rudimentary power and transport systems had often been re-established.

It seemed that the islanders had not so much lost their earlier technologies as lost faith in them. That the world we'd left behind had been discredited rather than destroyed.

The people here still left us entirely to our own devices, though we sensed that whatever remaining furniture they owned had been moved back – half as if they expected some kind of floor show, half in case we decided to smash everything in our path.

But since the islanders didn't actively move us on, and we ourselves felt no time pressure, our stays began to lengthen. And then we began to pick up certain changes in their attitudes.

Our presence appeared to unnerve them less. It was as if they'd been warned they might find us intrusive, even irritating. But we sensed they quite liked us giving them a reason to feel mildly peeved for the duration of our stay, before we continued to take care of the travelling.

The burden on each local community can't have been large.

There may by this stage have been an obligation for them to supply and service the residential blocks; also to carry out our boats' regular refits (or replacements – we didn't realize for quite some time what period pieces these were).

If there had to be a convoy passing through and putting down no roots – perhaps to signal the start of an era unblighted by the former generation's failures – then rather us than them: that's how we read their reasoning.

"Someone has to do it!" became our newest catchphrase.

I'd be stretched to pinpoint how and when we found out for sure that the blackout's harsh realities hadn't been entirely obliterated from their own memories, but this did appear to be the case.

Once nominal contact was established, we heard that one of their earliest nicknames for us was the Light Bringers.

Among ourselves we joked then that until our arrival in each new place, some lingering trace of the old blackout hadn't yet fully been dispersed. This would be met by more fusillades of that wild laughter from up on the downs. But though I've talked so far as if the state of suspension came to an end with the light's return, perhaps this wasn't so.

At the time we certainly thought in terms of a single zero hour, a point after which all would be reset. But maybe the broader process was much longer, continuing through the whole of this next phase, with the islanders sifting a new present from their past as they too worked out just how they wanted to evolve.

And I've often wondered since then whether by "light" those islanders may have actually meant "not loaded down"; not hidebound by the past in ways they themselves could never help but be.

It's possible we had some kind of totem value for them – totem or token – precisely on account of what we hadn't seen or done. If the world was to rise again (but "not in the old way" as so many islanders later phrased it), then were we adopted as mascots for whatever might be to come, good luck charms, carrying as we did no clear taint of the previous fall?

As a rule, however, we didn't dwell on any of the names they gave us. We knew they were out there, and if we happened to get wind of one, we'd smile but move on.

Coat People, Birds of Passage, Blank Tablets.

Land Gatherers, Bellwethers, Circus, Zeitgeist.

For so long uncertain if we were scapegoats or touchstones, successive groups of islanders understandably hedged their bets. To a degree, we were still hedging our own.

But if any of the names piqued our interest more than passingly, they tended to be musical. Chorus, Band, Orchestra. A handful of the boys called our stopovers "gigs". And although with each landfall we surely weren't putting into the world anything like actual light, sometimes when the gig boys pretended to be a real marching band, the space where their music might have been did not – as with the catchphrases – seem entirely empty.

I shouldn't jump ahead, but many years later a small boy would say to me, 'What's inside music? If the bit we hear is just the skin of it, the scent, what's the actual whole of music?'

There wasn't a great deal I could say to him in reply. Not then. But his question took me back to our expeditionary era, which did feel like a time of transaction as well as transition.

Could we, just conceivably, have been bringing something to leave behind? And might we also have been taking something on?

iv

Our own personal names were as negotiable as the group's, given and swapped on a regular basis, thrown up in the air like deck quoits to see which ones dropped down most fittingly around whom. No one had to live with a name they didn't like, especially the few that survived from the time before.

"Reger" was one we brought with us out of the dark. Brought by me, with increasingly little else.

I carried that name as a sound, a heard echo rather than a seen shape. A distant, fading adult female voice close to my ear calling it, cooing it.

"Rayga" was how it sounded, and before Lani made it over for me (or if ever I'd had a reason to write it down), that's how I'd have spelled it. I don't remember any of the others taking issue. Reger was just who I was. As the member of our grand collective answering to coat and locker number 31, the word "I" seemed the less smooth fit.

I should stress at this point that while some people's lives cry out for a memoir, mine doesn't. As will become clear, I'm writing this now only because I was directed to, and it can only be seen as my own personal take on a cycle of events we all lived through. So if these few pages should ever see the light of day, they'd ideally form part of a larger, more sophisticated book of *ours*: my own little lump of rock amid the marvellous archipelagos.

But since I was there, I can at least speak for myself by way of illustration: so when I say I brought "increasingly little else" from the previous era, here is the sum total of my memories:

I was somewhere out of bounds, sitting so hunched up beneath a workbench that my bare waxy knees were pressed to my face, and I was laughing hysterically as a man above planed a wooden block, his shavings cascading down through an opening in the bench like a rain of blond corkscrew feathers, until in the end I was drowning in a sea of wood. All I could see of the man was his legs, which at one point I clung to, pleading with him to stop, but only because I was laughing so hard I couldn't breathe.

The past can fall open anywhere, and that's where it fell for me. Little enough to go on, with a setting that's hardly "royal".

I never spoke of it to the others. None of them shared similar moments with me – and hand on heart, I'm not sure any of us lost sleep because so little punched its way through the veil.

In this as in much else, we were all past masters at not asking questions. Life seemed to be smiling on us: why rock the boats?

It wasn't as if our common amnesia held us back in any immediately practical ways. We still knew how to use dried peyote buttons, and which mushrooms to pick for the properties we were after. We just had little to no recall of our blood relatives. ('Maybe we didn't have any!' the rowdiest of our rowdy element, Tchure, would laugh. 'Maybe we were grown!')

We saw no reason even to ask where we were, though the answer to that may not have been simple. 'Archipelagonia!' is what Lani and I called our new world in private, scratching it in the sand and laughing: an incantatory kind of a word like Abracadabra, that came with its own exclamation mark. It seemed to fit.

And when, very cautiously, the islanders began to interact with us, for the most part they continued to take us on our own terms. At some locations we'd be directed to low-key welcome receptions in draughty public halls – usually, through organizational slippage, held closer in time to our departure.

There'd be cold sausage rolls in clear plastic containers, grain alcohol, paper plates weighed down by crumbly wedges of home-made jam sponge, a few neutral words from a spokesperson. We would be polite, wolf back more food and drink than we really wanted, then make our excuses.

Maybe from the way we looked and behaved, some elderly islanders assumed we really were on our way to college. "The" college they'd call it, as if there were just the one, the same way they'd talk of "the" blackout, and any residual jurisdiction in this fractured world as "the" authority.

In time, dignitaries from the latter group, usually women or people of indeterminate gender, would surface to offer small parties of us short local tours of inspection: bone-rattling truck rides from crumbling historic landmark to art treasure to the latest part-built call centre or reinstated pylon.

"This is as far as we were able to take things," our often-preoccupied guides seemed to tell us with their eyes, some of them looking as if they weren't quite ready to step aside.

We were on hand too as security became less tight – turnpike signs and rail station nameplates being restored, people starting to call certain key islands by their names again and not just cryptic letters of the alphabet – while what generally became known as the regrowth gathered pace.

And if we wanted it, there was work for us to do.

We weren't certain why these jobs were offered. It could have been part of some larger deal struck with the communities we were billeted on. At our blocks when we arrived, once the local economies allowed for it, there'd often be a printed sheet giving temporary employment options, alongside a list of outlets – bars mainly – where earnings might be spent.

The posts required little skill. Shelf-stacking, leaf-blowing, manning turnpike tollbooths; an extra pair of hands at a demolition site or crèche, fetching and carrying at archaeological digs before foundations could be laid for a new housing project.

At times the work seemed created purely for us to do, and none of it was compulsory, but most of us tried our hands. Perhaps we were meant to watch the islanders and learn. And why not? Most of them had been around a lot longer than us; in many cases their minds were quite obviously sharper.

Contact between them and us stayed minimal, with any conversation as good as meaningless. At times we had to wonder if we spoke the same language.

But from the outset we'd notice some of them, by contrast, watching us. The way a patient watches a doctor. Searching for clues, glancing up from the muddled heap of jigsaw pieces they saw within themselves to the picture on the box lid which – we slowly came to realize – they'd decided to see in us.

Perhaps our sheer naïvety put us nearer, in their eyes, to what everyone is born knowing, to whatever inhabits the innermost reptilian brain. "Unfingermarked" a spokesperson was heard to murmur at one particularly stilted wharfside reception. We had "unfingermarked hearts", she said.

Tchure and his sidekicks riffed heavily on that afterwards, firing off cracks about our "mission" to the islands. Soon, they'd say, we would be going out among these people with a view to introducing them to all the rest of our organs.

But in the event it was the people who came among us.

V

We'd reached our largest landmass so far. It turned out still to be an island, but for five consecutive days all we did was hug its southern shores, heading from one port of call to the next.

On the fifth evening, the step-change took place.

Though the urban hinterland here looked advanced, our block's locker area was especially gaunt. Just four primitive-looking showers at its thinly-concreted far end, so we boys stood around kicking our heels while the girls washed first.

When our turn came, the water was still warm enough to get up a good lather. The usual horseplay kicked in, and it was only then that we noticed we were being watched.

We'd heard girls' laughter, the shrill nervy sort that borders on a scream. We heard too the pin-drop stillness between each volley.

It wasn't our girls but islanders, half a dozen of them, just visible to us inside the dressing-room shadows. They knew we'd seen them but stood their ground. A couple then stepped closer:

steady-eyed girls not much younger than ourselves, still dressed in sober day-job uniforms. Nurses or shopworkers.

This was unheard of. No one outside of the group had ever set foot on "our" ground. Most of us boys queuing up with our towels immediately froze, but some of those under the fast-cooling jets matched the girls for bravado, mugging back, throwing exaggerated comic shapes.

Then one of the girls came closer still, tall in tapered black trousers, her eyes and mouth still too large for her heavily-freckled face, hands sunk deep in the pockets of a white nylon tunic: a deer stepping up to the hunter.

Such confidence, she had. Like a prosecuting counsel she leaned back a little, drawing her tunic tighter round herself, and her huge eyes swept over us before coming to rest on the boy beneath the left-hand central shower.

Frick was his name, the polished dome of his well-shaped hairless head under the thunder of the water jets making him stand out even more than usual.

Amid all the steam and murk, an arc light could now have been picking out just these two.

Frick didn't flinch. Turning, he faced the girl full on with the backs of his wrists on his hips, his pubic area and short thick penis all but obscured by foam.

The girl had chosen well, singling out someone with more than enough devilment of his own.

The foam slid lower, the girl smiled, Frick smiled back.

Our own girls were nowhere, although even in these few moments that pulsed like hours, some of us boys must surely have been wondering if they had actually set this up, if their abrupt disappearance before it began had been as definitive a signal as standing up in a boat to herald an island.

To still more incredulous shrieks from her gang, the young woman stepped on to the concrete.

There she hunkered down, balancing on the balls of her bare feet, and swung both slim knees to one side.

Her lips were no more than an arm's length from Frick's tensed thigh. Soaked through now by his shower, she craned her neck further forward. Then she tilted her face around, and to gasps from everyone, when a fat wad of foam fell away from between Frick's legs, she caught most of it in her mouth.

She stood without wiping off the spillage, the other island girls squealing so loudly that they couldn't have heard what she said before they – and even the most fazed of us – applauded her all the way out.

I'd been well within hearing range, though.

"All present and correct," was the verdict she delivered with clear satisfaction in her voice. "Definitely all there."

I don't recall any other islanders ever stepping inside one of our perimeter fences – not *as* islanders – though for a while we must constantly have been on the lookout in case they did.

The start of the assimilation, such as it turned out to be, can't categorically be dated from this episode. But that girl must have made some sort of a perforation, leaving the fields of "us" and "them" no longer so distinct.

From that point on, if we wanted to be, we were out of the blocks. And not too long afterwards, "hybrid" couples began to form – which was also when we got to hear how promiscuous the islanders had until then presumed we were.

vi

The general island view seemed to be that along with our unfingermarked hearts, we were all unbridled children of nature. Though I'd say this was some way off the mark, I wouldn't want to overstress our innocence either.

From the moment the light returned, a sexual charge was palpably there between us, and it went on building – largely unconducted, hedged about by ever-keener curiosity – until in the end, after our possibly aborted epiphany up on the downs, our instincts led us into forming pairs, by no means all of them heterosexual, and few of them strictly exclusive.

This isn't now the simplest thing to explain, as I found out many years later during my series of official hearings.

Among ourselves we'd use the word "pairs", since "couples" was reserved for liaisons with islanders. But before these pairings began, we had all more or less grown up together. We weren't exactly family, but maybe a sense of that lingered. (We called it "twinning" as well as pairing up, though I think this was a play on an arrangement towns or cities of a certain size used to make with their equivalents in other countries.)

Each of us was always his or her own person, but part of our condition seemed to be the ready acceptance of boundaries: if we really were an orchestra, then it was a self-conducting one.

Most of us freely used drugs, for instance, but we'd draw the line at anything hard. So when it came to fooling around, we used our ingenuity, which could generate its own excitements (a lot of seed was spilled, and if the rowdies were to be believed, even more of it swallowed), but I'd be surprised if any pair went as far as what Tchure used to call "full reproductive intercourse" or F.R.I.

What's certain is that no one ever had a baby – or, as far as I'm aware, a termination, which may in turn have helped feed a more lurid set of island rumours, that we'd been left sterile by some form of experimentation during the blackout.

If this all sounds tentative, I'm afraid that's how we were. Exploratory yet inhibited. We knew what to do sexually. There was just this confusion over who we might do it with.

Confusion is a word that covers so much of our existence in this phase. We still knew so little about anything.

Yet as we continued to ride our luck, there really seemed to be no pressing reason to make ourselves any better informed.

After the incident in the shower some of us even got it into our heads that thus far we had only really been going through the motions ("practising") until one day we'd be ready to give the whole of ourselves to strangers.

It may perhaps be most helpful to think of our pairings as two wheels on a single axle: joined, but always at a distance.

But here's the vital element. Although each of us would be creating something truly singular with one other person, this took nothing away from the wider cohort. Rather, it helped make that larger vehicle run more smoothly. (And just as the uncanny pallor of the downland heart of light might have been said to derive from all our own colours passed back through a prism, so each new pair seemed to make us much more than the sum of our parts.) At least this was my own experience, especially with Lani.

By the time of Frick's shower moment, Lani and I had already become well established as a pair. Before me, she'd actually been with Frick – the clipped, polished way they both spoke suggesting similar original backgrounds – and she still spent a lot of time in his company as well as mine.

Lani (pronounced Lahnee) was a name she'd made up for herself, as opposed to a "real" one, though in a world where most of us picked with a pin the dates when we celebrated our own birthdays, such distinctions were seldom clear-cut.

She'd given herself a host of different names. Mahonia, Roseblade, Maquette – "Lani" was, however, one of those thrown-up quoits that seemed to drop down particularly snugly around her tall, spare frame: Lani in her trademark suede shade-of-avocado coat with its nicotine-yellowed ocelot collar, its hemline hovering above her latest pair of spike-heeled ankle boots.

We said very soon we loved each other. Lani wouldn't just say or whisper it, she'd scrawl it too with her toe in the hard dark sand at low tide. This sand-writing was quite a thing with her; we'd gaze down at her words, trading freighted silences.

But I don't recall her speaking to me one-to-one before we got together. I once heard – it must've been from Frick – that the way I looked unsettled her. ('I didn't mean your appearance,' she later protested. 'We all look great. It's more of a look in your eyes when you're making one of your jokes.' Back in the early days no one tired quicker than Lani of my admittedly hit-and-miss sense of humour.)

None of this matters in itself. Over time we formed dozens of pairs inside the cohort, scores of them, whether serial or overlapping. Lani matters here because long before twinning with me, she had taken on responsibility for "the book".

As far back as I remember, one or another of our girls kept what we boys understood to be a cohort log.

Among themselves the girls referred to this simply as "the book" or "book of ours", and it seemed to belong very firmly in the female domain.

Whether or not keeping it updated was a formal obligation is unclear. None of the rest of us ever tried to see what was written. All we'd know was that at each stopover, the basic equipment for longhand writing would appear in the relevant person's locker, and during the stay we would see her intermittently take herself off to fill in a few notebook pages. Then, when we moved on, the log would be left behind.

However it was that each girl came to get the job, I recall at least five or six of them doing it before Lani, but she was the only one I ever heard talk about it.

vii

Ostensibly Lani was the most conscientious of the book keepers, taking her writing tools up onto lonely clifftops where as well as fulfilling her quota of words, she'd sit and smoke, alone, for hours on end, facing the western sea with its thousand roads and appearing to track each one through to wherever it might lead.

There were times, even within our little troop of nomads, when Lani could appear especially displaced. During her deepest withdrawals she almost seemed to go missing from herself.

None of the girls who wrote held down beer-money jobs during their stint, and not all of us could have handled so much of our own company.

The few times I myself strayed out of immediate contact with the group I soon lost confidence. Just to think of the phrase we later used when referring to a recent leaver – "no longer of the party" – could make my shoulders prickle with unease.

Lani was made of sterner stuff, but the work still didn't seem to bring her much joy. Nor did the deep interest she took, island by island, in the local barracks children.

We gave that name to these small kids since usually they were corralled into compounds that once housed garrisons. We thought they came from service families, but finally pieced together that at the age of five all the island young were taken from their homes and given into the care of female educators. I've already mentioned "not in the old way" – the islanders' own call to action, and soon we would be seeing the NITOW acronym daubed on walls and bridges – but for us this was some of the earliest evidence of how it was put into practice.

The children were always strikingly clean and enjoyed a fair amount of freedom. On some islands, groups of them took to staking out our blocks, watching us come and go.

In time the more curious ones formed orderly blocs at the wharves for our dawn departures. Older islanders might be on hand at our arrivals but only the barracks children ever watched us go, as if they needed to confirm we really were leaving. (Tchure once made us laugh by suggesting there was a cull wherever we stopped over, with just the kids left standing by the time we moved on. We hooted even more at his idea that we ourselves were being "fattened up" for "eventual slaughter".)

It was at these dawns that we had our first sighting of the small luminous marks, presumably painted on before they went to bed, that a few of the barracks children wore at both temples. A pale glowing flash in the rough shape of a heart.

The first time Lani spoke to me about the book, I had gone to fetch her – perched out on a rocky coastal outcrop – for our evening meal. She shook her head vehemently and made me sit with her and watch what was going on below.

A column of barracks children some way to her left was being marched along the shore by two black-gowned minders until they reached a mudflat exposed by a receding tide which would soon be coming back in.

None of the children in the group looked older than eight or nine. We couldn't quite hear what the minders were saying to them, and while one of the women tied a blindfold around the first, Lani grew tense and leaned in so close that strands of her plume of black hair tickled my ear.

In turn the minder then blindfolded all the obedient children.

As each one stepped gingerly towards the water's edge, arms outreached like a sleepwalker's, the minders would clap in time, calling out numbers in a countdown, or count-up, which would end when the child ground to a halt and ripped off the blindfold.

Some managed no more than a staggering step or two. A few looked inconsolable afterwards. Then a skinny little boy didn't stop at all, breaking rather into a purposeful blind trot towards the incoming tide, almost flying as he broke the first ripples, racing up shallow stairs in the air then collapsing headlong into the spume as he tore off the knotted scarf.

Even after the minders had shepherded all the children out of our sight, my heart was still rapping against my ribs from the impact made by that boy's sheer zest.

'Their parents had to let them go,' said Lani, and when I turned to her, I saw tears snaking down her oval face.

She'd always had her moments, but her more public crying jags were full of a fury missing here. I didn't dare ask, but had to wonder if what we'd just seen had triggered some incident from her own lost childhood.

I might have tried to console her just by quipping, 'We used to know that'. Instead I drew her closer still, so the gorgeous ripe fug of her green coat swaddled us both.

She reached up and touched the hank of hair I now wore gathered in a fat rubber band at the nape of my neck. 'Wait a moment,' she said. 'Wait while I finish.'

She picked up her writing materials, then edged far enough away to stop me from seeing what was going on to the page.

It wasn't just a moment I waited, more like an hour.

For much of it Lani hardly used her pen at all, just peered out hard at the horizon. She'd make occasional passes at the paper, a line of words here, a couple more there, as if she was trying to draw from life a person approaching across the waves, someone who was still so distant she couldn't yet work out if she wanted them any closer or not.

On finally snapping the notebook shut, still eyeing the water, she seemed on the point of weeping again.

'It doesn't get any easier,' she said.

'The log?'

She rolled her eyes. 'It's only you boys who call it that! Probably because you can't see anything that isn't sitting right in front of you, crying out to be described!'

'Then what is it you're writing?'

She dipped her head. 'Oh, whatever comes to us. Then they can take out of it whatever it is they want.'

She'd lost me. 'Well,' I said, 'you're the writer.'

'Rider, rather.' She sighed, then smiled. 'Surfer. It's all out there already, coming at us in waves. I just ride in on its back.'

She fussed at a strap on her ankle boot before rising. When she looked across at me her smile had become more forced.

'But what we write is probably immaterial. It's how we write it.'

viii

With one standout exception that I'll soon be coming to, during our time together neither Lani nor I had hybrid relationships with islanders too. A growing number of the rest of us did, though.

Frick spent a week at the flat of the girl who'd entered our shower, but before we moved on he came back alone, his old swagger slightly dented. 'I don't mind telling you, Reger,' was as much as he'd let on (loudly enough for Lani beside me in the boat to hear), 'our own sexual relations are in their infancy!'

Others would stay away for longer, then return with their island lovers. Sometimes, too, they'd already ceased to be a couple, but the islander still joined us. In a way, we were prepared for new additions. At our blocks there had always been more numbered lockers than people in the cohort.

No one who wanted to come was turned away.

Each new recruit – and by the time I had to stop counting, these made up around one in ten of our number – would say they'd been waiting for us all along, that they too remembered only dark seclusion from before. Some would tell us they'd found a number, always higher than ninety, inked on to an item of their original clothing.

It was almost as if they had once been with us, during the blackout perhaps, then re-emerged at farther-flung points out to sea. But each one came to be with all of us, not just the person who'd been their initial contact. They would then become part of the larger procession: a stronger procession too, in no way diluted. Each change seemed to add to our sense of momentum.

There were also, in time, some original cohort members who left the blocks to follow their hearts and never came back.

Each withdrawal would be registered in the same way: the rest of us finding at dawn the latest leaver's coat draped ritually across an opened locker door, with her (to start with, it was always one of our steadier girls) photo pinned to its material.

The photo had its own shock value. From whatever disparate places we'd been sprung, nobody thought mirrors – let alone cameras – had been there, and finding not so much as a looking glass in the blocks, we must tacitly have agreed to go on "unreflected", girls and boys alike. At least that was the unspoken ideal. Maybe an element of superstition was involved.

When shaving, or more likely putting on eye-shadow, most of us thought we could see enough in our locker doors, buffed up to a sheen with our coat-sleeves. But there were definite gains to be made by looking more intently at one another. We became our own mirrors, every one of us seeing something vitally unique about everybody else (just as, once we'd had enough shared experiences, we could help to fill in each other's memories until at last the forgetting stopped).

Usually the leaver's image would be a cheap instant-camera shot, taken by whichever islander our girl had opted to quit the boats and settle down with. This – each snapshot seemed to be saying – is how I now wish to be seen, the way I look to just one other, the one who matters to me most.

We'd stand by the lockers, passing around the low-resolution photo, sometimes not immediately recognizing the face. The subject would look so happy, with perhaps a hint of personal amazement, as if she had vaulted on ahead of the camera flash and seen herself too, finally and for the first time.

To our minds there was no longer the same light in their eyes. They'd look less young – more hidebound? – now that they had taken this next irreversible step, which could just as easily have been a step back or sideways as forwards.

Because they could no longer hear us, the abusive tirade we'd then unleash at the photo continued until we felt secure that although we had all in effect just been dumped, the truer loser was this blameless, seemingly prematurely-aged girl.

And once our invective had run its course, we'd feel better primed to travel on again together, knowing ourselves only through one another. Works still in progress, eggs waiting to be hatched, as we saw it, not snatched from out of the pan.

'We'll have no truck with island men!' our girls with their heads tilted back would holler into the vaults of the ocean sky, filled to so stupendous a height with bright shining air. ("Island cock" was the actual phrase, but at this distance it's probably kinder not to relay word for word our unformed younger selves' everyday language, as provisional as everything else about us.)

One morning I remember lying stretched out with Lani in a pinnace we had entirely to ourselves while louder girls chanted in the boats all around. We were both smiling up at the heavens, and just for an instant I thought I could see what else was so huge – in us, for us, because of us – that there had to be so vast a space to hold it all.

Then it was gone, but it had been here.

So still was Lani, preparing to pit herself once more against the book. 'Another day, another magpie,' she would say, having identified the black-and-white bird as her spirit-creature long before she'd settled on her own name.

'Don't they say one for sorrow, two for joy?' I asked soon after we got together. 'Maybe we should have a magpie each?'

'No I'm sorry, there's only one,' Lani shot back. 'And it's mine.'

ix

Early one afternoon I found her kneeling on a patch of pebble-ringed sand down near that island's wharf, dressed in a pretty pink cotton top and jeans. Going closer, I saw she had written a name in stringy capitals with one of the stones: *REGER.*

I'd never thought of it spelled that way, but I nodded. Next to it she then inscribed a heart, but instead of going on to write her own name, she hauled herself upright on my arm.

'And I might be Bead now,' she said.

Bead, I thought. Something small, holed and rounded which didn't make too much sense unaccompanied.

'Or it could be a name for you,' she went on softly. 'All that beady-eyed watching you do, to fuel your awful jokes!'

With the sole of her boot she scuffed out the last "R" of REGER, and with its toe she adapted the first "R" into a "B". Then she scratched a "D" around the "G".

'"Bede"?' I read, still seeing the beaded loop of thread. I was drawn to the look of this newer word, its internal balance; our names always had as much to do with shape as sound or meaning. I saw myself strung together with the others in a rosary, one tiny prayer among the many. But I was "Reger".

Lani slipped the pebble she'd been writing with into my hand. A rose-flecked white, shaped like an irregular heart.

'New name for a new start?' she said in the same soft voice, and she ran two fingers down my scrubbily bearded cheek.

Turning the pebble in my palm and watching her glide away, notebook and pen in hand, I had a hunch she was about to call time on our pairing. I could not have been more wrong.

It may also be wrong to suggest that a greater sense of familiarity was beginning to lead certain islanders to take against us – not that we didn't often make ourselves appear total fools, holy or otherwise.

We might spend whole mornings chasing squirrels, or play frisbee for hours in the pitch darkness; we still wore our coats when there was no earthly need to. This sort of thing could in certain cases appear transparently self-conscious, even affected, which may have tried some islanders' patience. Others may not have shared our romantic hope that if and when the regrowth really hit its stride, every last person would benefit to the same extent.

There was never outright hostility, not then, and still nothing on our route seemed chargeable. We continued to be – if we were anything at all to them – their designated drifters. Yet a few of us had started to feel we were no longer quite such free agents.

'It's us who make you tick!' a drunken convenience-store manager laughed at us across the embers of one welcoming committee's beach barbecue. She said it over and over, even while she was being hustled away by her colleagues, as if received wisdom decreed it to be the other way round. We smiled and couldn't disagree. (It was never our purpose to be disagreeable.)

'You think the world's fallen in your lap!' she shouted. 'But what if it doesn't turn out any better next time?'

Elsewhere we heard gibes about a "levy" or a "tribute", which possibly referred to a supporting tax, but at times appeared to mean us – all of us – as a kind of enlisted group.

This went deeper than the mild peevishness I referred to before. The island people made us tick – that's what at least a proportion of them thought. They wound us up then kept us going, and no one makes a clock tick for the clock's own sake. A clock or a bomb.

We were offered fewer tours of inspection too, until in the end these were discontinued – in hindsight, understandably.

The last time I volunteered for a tour party, we were taken to a thousand-year-old temple. According to our short-breathed male guide, its buttery stone, quarried nearby, knew how to soak up and store the sunshine. High above one aisle was a range of "corbels", crudely-carved fantastical creatures whose erotic postures set us all off on rounds of helpless sniggering.

The guide could only stand and wait for us to finish, rubbing at his chest as if to ward off a heart attack.

'Nothing is really new, don't you see?' he said, struggling to mask what must have been deep-seated scepticism. 'Not really.'

On other tours one of us might murmur, 'We used to know that', possibly our most annoying catchphrase, though it wasn't always as facetious as it may have sounded to our guides.

It didn't even have to relate to hard fact. We might be sitting under a café awning when a breeze whipped up the corner of the thin paper sheet clipped to our table. The waitress's raised eyebrow, then, as she re-fixed it, the reek of old rain, the nearby chink of fork on plate: all these would be registered, and when the waitress went away, one or another of us would nod. 'What just happened,' we'd say with a wave of the hand to truss up the whole moment. 'We used to know that.'

It could've been true. A random foothold in the time we'd left behind, when all that most of us could recall was being sectioned off, quarantined. Or it could've been more complicated.

Soon after the tours stopped, I was travelling by funicular railway with Tchure and two others to work on a clifftop track extension. Two young local women started talking to us. It interested them, they said, that we as a cohort had been on the move for so long.

'Is it to gather up every last person who's meant to be with you,' asked one of them with unusual directness, 'and set down every last one who isn't? Until you reach a kind of critical mass?'

Her almond-shaped eyes were fixed on mine, but it was Tchure who asked her back in his equally direct way, 'Until we're all present and correct, you mean?'

The young woman smiled distantly, at me, and that was that. But her idea of our complement rising or falling to its perfect final size was as good a way as any to measure our progress.

Tchure and the others kept bringing up the way that girl and I had looked at each other. In dreams I kept seeing her half-knowing eyes, her body rocking to the car's rhythm. My own rocking too. I'd imagine myself going back home with her at the end of that day. In another life I might have.

Yet if I'd felt able to say anything at all to her, it would have been 'I used to know that'. Not "we" but for the first time ever, truly, "I". Her straight-backed posture and half-swallowed smile, her not-quite-convincing air of primness: it all seemed eerily familiar.

Perhaps a desire I was not at that point ready to do anything about had pushed her, even at first glance, into a part of my heart which I could only safely describe as memory.

Nor can I say that I knew we would one day meet again. It wasn't that kind of a feeling at all. More as if we'd been together already, and even back then too much history had come between us. What made it all the more confounding was that Tchure, watching us so closely, had seemed to be aware of this too.

X

I've mentioned Tchure several times, and for a reason. He was soon to play a key part in ending this phase of the cycle – and who knows what else after? There were also traits in him that to a degree ran through the whole cohort, and since there isn't space to do justice to every individual member, I'll say a little more about him here as a way of pointing up the general picture.

Not as tall as some, he went about in a dapper frock-coat which accentuated his stockiness. I'm not sure we had the term "hyperactive" then, but that conveys some of his flavour.

He could barely stay still. We'd see him skip, jump, bob and weave on his pre-dawn jogs before a departure. He'd approach at speed across a beach or dressing room, grinning in a way that forced you to grin back, then pepper the space around you with a flurry of faux martial-arts kicks and jabs.

You could almost hear the crackle in his frame, his limbs screaming out for excuses to be used. He seemed desperate to stretch and claw his way into an altogether bigger space, as if he knew he had to live his life twice as fast the rest of us. His wide, mildly pitted face would be similarly restless, often flaring up in expressions his features didn't quite seem able to frame.

He amused the girls, both ours – including Lani, who'd paired with him before Frick – as well as plenty more from the islands. (One of the first things any of us remembered him saying was that line about our task being to repopulate the planet, which almost certainly wasn't his own.) There he'd be, prowling the corner of a block compound: up and down, up and down, grunting as if to himself, flicking his wrists like towels. But invariably there was a girl sitting in a nearby doorway, chin propped on her raised knees, waiting for him to be done: whatever it was that Tchure did.

There was a less benign side too. I didn't see either incident myself, but in two separate dorms he worked himself up into such a frenzy that it took four or five other boys to wrestle him to the ground until it passed. Both times he'd been flipping an electric light switch off and on, faster and faster, apparently in the hope of "getting to see what the dark really looked like".

Both times he blew all the fuses.

One evening, returning late to the block after a long run, I got to witness a more abstruse outburst on my own.

From some distance I saw Tchure standing braced against an outside wall, stripped to the waist, his whole upper body convulsing. Concerned for him, I hurried closer, only to realize he was hurling all his energy into a stream of curses: such unalloyed depravity that it stopped me dead in my tracks.

Even from behind I saw this wasn't anger or frustration but a rabid sort of arousal, windmilling his arms, running a gamut of obscene gestures with his fingers. It was a one-man show, a war-dance – and a countdown surely to his own total implosion.

But Tchure did not implode.

He leapt up and swung around.

Crouching now, fists balled, he leered up at me, still spitting profanities. It was infantile, ecstatic, more alien than anything I'd ever seen on our travels – and for an instant I was back on the downs, seeing as if through an islander's eyes this rawness, which so many of our number had in them too. So *this* was us.

But still I found myself nodding along to Tchure's deep, wrenched-up beat, the sweet and filthy pulse of it, because equally deep within I knew this was how we were supposed to feel.

Perhaps that's why I can't now recall an end to Tchure's crazed explosive hymn that day. In its way it pounds on still. All I could do was witness it: this thing in Tchure, and in so many of the others – maybe in all of them – that didn't seem to be in me.

Not when I was on my own.

If Tchure took to extremes a tendency within our group, so too did Lani. Like him she could always turn heads, but where he was all extravert activity, she'd plumb her own depths.

Shortly before she changed everything between us, she carefully closed her notebook after what must have been another difficult session and said to me, 'Precision shrinks things, don't you think? It's like looking through a gun-sight, narrowing down the world to the thing you're going to kill.'

Then she swung around to raise and aim an imaginary rifle out to sea from our spit of land, the position of her hands suggesting this was something she knew exactly how to do.

I'm not saying everyone in the cohort thought and spoke like that, but a number of them did. Boys as well as girls.

And I don't want to make Lani sound precious or morose. She could laugh as hard as anyone, most often when it was just the two of us. (At times my jokes still got her down, but she did enjoy hearing me mimic the others' voices to say outrageous things.)

Lani's long hours of thought perhaps made her an ideal contributor to the "book of ours", although this responsibility may itself have fuelled her introspectiveness. So when she tried to transfer the responsibility to me, I was initially lost for words.

'Your turn now,' was all she said, pressing on me the notebook and pen she'd just taken from her latest locker. Then, with a firm squeeze to the front of my jeans as a parting shot, she waltzed away to sign up for a garden clearance.

Until we reconnected that evening I carried around both items as if they were radioactive. 'No, they're yours!' she protested when I tried to hand them back. 'I've said as much as I can now. And besides, we've only ever been keeping them warm for you.' (The word she used was definitely "we".)

'You don't just have to be the class clown,' she pointed out. 'You notice things. Writing could bring out that side: show you who you really are. Your pen name could be Bede!'

Her eyes lit up as gently she disengaged her limbs from mine.

'You've got to reach past yourself,' she said. 'We all have. It's what we're for.'

She made it sound like a tease, the way Lani made many things sound, and it was hard to keep a straight face back. For the rest of that short stay I didn't risk writing a word. ('I'm no writer!' I kept telling her under my breath. 'Write-off, perhaps.') I even doubted Lani was allowed to just opt out, though for all I knew each of the girls before her had nominated her own successor.

But on reaching the next island, it was in locker number 31, my own, that the writing materials turned up. (Always a thin ring-bound A5 pad with "NOTEBOOK" stamped on its bendy transparent cover; each pen white with a small tapering royal-blue section toward the nib, full of ink yet old, the lettering of a charity's name all but worn away from its circular shaft.)

The same happened at every subsequent stop.

Nobody, then or later, contested my right to the role. Someone had to do the work. The person now was me.

xi

I don't suppose I took it as seriously as I might've. No one had ever looked to me for seriousness. Nor was I seriously funny like Tchure. His edgier flights of fancy (like his insistence to many of our island hosts that we were shielding an intellectually-gifted boy called Kuno who refused to wear clothes or feed himself) were central to our cohort's canon.

My own "class clowning" was more lightweight. But if my jokes were never going to pass into comic folklore, people did at least look to me for ready quips, which – as a person still a little haunted by having been the last one to laugh up there inside the heart of light – I have to admit I found reassuring.

So, unlike the girls who'd been responsible for the book before me, I saw no need to hive myself off. I'd stay around each block, happy to be distracted if anything else was going on.

I'd always lacked the patience to read. How now to write?

For a while I did as Lani had suggested any boy would, describing whatever was right in front of me. I soon gave up asking her what I might put down instead.

'It has to come from you!' she'd say while gleefully grabbing my arm. 'It's all yours now'. 'You could think of it as a love letter,' was her last ever tip, without smiling this time. 'To the person you'll one day most want to share everything with.'

In time I started putting pen to paper without a thought in my head, trying out sentences or single words, just to see how they looked. What emerged, to my surprise, was fairly low on comedy.

Sweating under the sun in my black and by now buttonless greatcoat, fuelled by a flagon of the latest local grain alcohol, I'd half-hallucinate that the actual words weren't my main business, that what mattered were the twists and turns of my wrist, even the soft creak and scuffle of the pen as it formed the letters.

Or else – taking a cue from what Lani had said about riding in or surfing – I'd tell myself the words were already there on the pages ("pre-scribed") so all I had to do was ape the sequence of shapes and sounds that had gone into their prescription.

At other times still I simply drew the light-form we'd seen on the downlands. Page after page, version after version, until I was satisfied that this was what had appeared to us, before we all went up into it.

And while what I produced most often called to mind the shape of a heart, on some days it came out closer to the strung void of a harp, although always – essentially – it was both.

Once I was in this kind of zone, I began to think differently about our journey, and to notice things that had perhaps long been obvious to the others. Like the fact that not more than one couple ever seemed to form per island – the respective partners usually becoming involved soon after disembarkation.

One of us, a boy now as often as a girl, would be drawn to someone on the island's semi-official reception committee. In due course they'd go off, then the rest of us hung fire until we'd learn how things had panned out.

Yet even before we landed there'd be a growing sense of whose turn had come; an awareness as the boats neared the shore that a particular boy or girl had now entered the frame.

It made me wonder if this awareness was in itself enough to make all the rest happen. I also wondered if our hosts had prior knowledge of who might emerge from their own number.

Occasionally older islanders would approach if they saw me in a certain spot near the block on consecutive days. Whether or not they had been assigned to do so, they'd volunteer stories which I later wrote up just as they were told to me.

A woman taking time out from digging clams said she'd once been a postmistress. She explained what used to happen to local people suspected of "collaboration" during their blackout. They would be set adrift in a rowboat with a little food and water, and a hammer-shaped tool to beat off big seabirds.

'There were plenty of other islands a person might fetch up on,' she told me. 'D'you see, this was a death penalty that mightn't turn out to be a death penalty. For a person who mightn't actually have been a criminal.' She flung her arms wide. 'We just let them go!'

On the way out of one reception event, a middle-aged man on that evening's committee slipped a folded sheet into my coat pocket: a printed list of all the "comestibles" supplied, with the number of each item in brackets after it. Vashti said he'd come up and asked her as soon as we arrived who "the writer" was.

I should say here, however, given what came later, that no one ever brought up a "lighterman" with me. I'm not even sure I knew, back then, that such a person figured in a traditional rhyme.

Inside the group, it wasn't as if the book's keeper had any special status. Writing was just what I did, in much the same way that one of our girls turned wood. While Ananke left behind her simple chairs, lampstands and corner units which the islanders would (we guessed) treat, finish and furnish their homes with, I would leave a few scribbled pages – though for a while yet we didn't know what, if anything, became of them.

And now that the writer was me, and so considered unavailable for more regular manual work, Lani by contrast was freed up to take on a series of outdoor jobs. She'd spend a day slashing back conifers, then despite furious showering stay sticky with resin for a week. Her coat would reek of sawdust and loam.

I didn't mind missing out on the beer money. When I wasn't with Lani I tended not to get wasted quite so often with the others anyway. I'd go instead for ever-longer coast path runs. There wouldn't be many islands I hadn't circled, several times, before we headed out. "Beating the bounds", Lani called it.

And still, like every other pair, we had to snatch any moments of intimacy al fresco (though the fuse stayed lit in between times, with Lani's caresses often seeming to bear fruit only later, like the seeds and bulbs she patted into the soil with her thin musician's fingers) until we came to an island where, tantalizingly briefly, all this changed.

xii

Instead of a block on this island, new wooden signposts directed us to a brand new authority-run "retreat" overlooking the sea.

Some of the girls likened the unoccupied mini-town (mostly made up of quaint two-person cabins) to places they'd read about called holiday camps. Each cabin held a week or so's provisions, while our lockers were located in a large central building with the look of an ocean liner, still festooned with scaffolding, which hoardings claimed would soon benefit from the construction of an underground sports complex.

Until now, I'd never spent a night inside with Lani. None of our pairs had, with all the block dorms designated for sleeping only. But while at this retreat, we were given the chance to live like true couples.

In many ways this was our high water mark.

I'd never known anything like lying spooned into Lani through the nights, feeling her steady heartbeat under my balled protective fist, seeing her stir from our bed in the mornings: her naked back as she twisted away to zip up a boot, the marvel of all that musculature shimmering and rippling just beneath her skin.

The evenings too were blissful, when we'd all lie spread-eagled in a kind of central plaza, competing to give obscene new names to the sharply-defined constellations. ('All those little hearts of light,' was the only thing Lani kept saying, just to me.) I'd pull her closer thinking, *So this is you*, meaning me as much as her, and everyone else as much as either of us. 'That's the meaning of the "the universe", right?' Miyake pointed out as we gazed up into infinity. 'All turned into one?'

And it seemed to be true. In these transcendent moments I didn't just have the feeling that we as a group were one. It went much further, enlarging on what I'd begun to sense on the downs: as if each of the countless worlds up there held infinitesimally different versions of ourselves, and every last one of those versions – with all of their triumphs and tragedies – was needed for the most perfect harmonic whole to be formed. We were close, so very close that I thought I picked up its first resonance.

On the last night, after a communal meal during which we'd all seemed not so much to be talking as creating a common new sound, I felt lifted up, to look down on us now as if from one of those alternative worlds, and with more curiosity than ever before I wondered what our distinguishing condition really was.

That we were "not quite right" had always seemed a given for the islanders. But in what way or ways were we wrong? And how might this have made us, in the eyes of some of them at least, more right than they saw themselves?

From above, I found few clues in the way we looked. Lani wasn't wrong: as a group the cohort was always easy on the eye. Even manchild Tchure with his pitted skin had an undeniable glamour.

Again, I could not quite isolate what set us apart. As far as I was able to see, our state, our condition, was simply one of being entranced – by one another, by this world that we found ourselves moving through, by whatever came at us.

As for Lani, if ever we now travelled on in separate boats, she said she felt new heat from my eyes. On the brink of sleep at nights I'd launch thoughts at her dorm that were the closest I ever came to praying.

'Archipelagonia!' we'd whisper to each other in a host of borrowed voices: the magic word of power we'd tied down to a place. I had sensed that our pairing was close to an end. Instead, like our larger journey, we just went on beginning – as if forever poised in the glorious open-sesame moment which exists between an evening's first two beers.

And then the offprints started to appear. Small 8- or 16-page leaflets stapled together inside blue sugar-paper covers.

Golovina found the first in a nearby seafront teashop, mixed in with that day's magazines and newspapers. She seemed more amused than amazed: 'It looks like poetry,' she told me. So did Sinclair when he found a half dozen copies of another stacked on the counter of a burger joint – free distribution, just one left by the time he got around to collecting his order.

Neither Golovina nor Sinclair (nor any others of us afterwards) gave an indication of having read them.

But here they now were, on respectfully numbered typeset pages: verbatim reproductions of passages I had written before sheepishly shoving them back inside earlier lockers.

It surprised me that anyone should have gone to the trouble of putting them through this low-key printing and distribution process. It all came under my name too; both names, in fact, even if I hadn't realized that anyone save Lani thought I had two.

Heart of Light it would say at the top of each left-hand page, *Reger Bede* at the top on the right.

Each column of text was quite narrow, with generous margins to either side. The proportions were pleasing – not much ink, a lot of blank space. I could see that it might look manageable: little islands of text in an ocean of white, despite the fact that screeds of it could have made no immediate sense.

Until these appeared – and whoever Lani once thought she'd been writing for – I had honestly imagined my scribbles were for my eyes only. I guessed the authority was having them printed up and circulated out of sheer curiosity value, to prove that at least one of us could get from one end of a sentence to another.

But for me, this put into a slightly different light something else we'd all laughed about while staying at the retreat, something Zhiyin had clearly saved up to tell us.

Several islands before, she'd been painting a fence adjoining the grounds of a barracks school, and had listened in on a few minutes of an open-air lesson for the older pupils. They were taking turns to read aloud extracts from pieces they'd all written.

Zhiyin couldn't know what they had been asked to produce – each child referred to the presumably common subject only as "They" – but by the time one of the minders spotted her, then ushered the class away to the shade of a more distant tree, she felt sure the task they'd been set was to describe our cohort.

At dinner that evening she closed her eyes and tried to recall some of the things she'd overheard.

"They're so centred in the moment that all time seems to gather round them," was one. Her favourite ran along the lines of, "Wherever they go, there's slowly moving light. Old-looking light that shows the rest of us at new angles to one another. It's like a game of musical chairs, played with alternating light and dark."

We soon went on to laugh about something else, something more coherent. I didn't know what to think myself, but again I felt those odd little pricklings of unease in my shoulders.

Several of the phrases, you see, were mine. From a slow day with the notebook months before, when I'd emptied my head and had one of my shots at automatic writing. That gathering of time, those musical chairs: these were what first came to me, as Lani might've put it, and then they came from me. Lani who'd

70

been sitting by my side as usual that mealtime, and had hardly laughed at all with the others.

Zhiyin said something else about the open-air barracks school lesson, tugging with a frown at her juju trinket braids:

'I may not have got this right, but it really did seem to be the kids doing the teaching, with the minders being taught.'

I waited and waited after that evening for Lani to bring up the offprints, but she never did. At least not with me.

None of this – none of it – was what I had been expecting.

Even now I'm hesitant to speak on behalf of the whole cohort, but maybe my own personal distinguishing condition was that I never had the first idea what was going to happen next.

xiii

The only one of us to die was found on an overcast afternoon – by islanders – just beyond the area of managed woodland which on many of the islands would border our residential blocks.

I'd been away that day, not writing but running, since for once I had managed to cover a couple of pages quite quickly. By the time I got back, most of the initial shock must already have been absorbed by the rest of the group.

On the cracked asphalt road leading up to the block, Sempra, a girl I'd once paired with, came out to head me off.

With a tender smile she took my arm and guided me along a rougher track to the place where the bodies had been discovered. That gave her a little time to fill me in.

'One of ours and one of theirs,' was the way she put it.

Local officials suspected no foul play; it appeared to have been a pact, carefully planned. 'Overdose,' said Sempra, giving me the name of some pills I'd not previously heard of.

At this point, our destination came into view: a small but steep, south-facing grass bank. Two female security officers sat watching over it. When they saw us they stood, and below them on the grass lay something that made my step falter.

A loose shape had been created by the intermittent placing of items of clothing, both male and female, ranging from boots and tights to a long silk scarf. I'm not sure I'd have been minded to call this shape that of a heart, or even a harp, had not three lengths of incident tape been pegged to the ground to surround it in just such a way.

Not all the female clothing was familiar to me, but the long green coat with its ocelot collar – the sole garment on display which was neither black nor white – could only have been Lani's.

'They were lying together inside the arrangement of clothes,' said Sempra, as I stepped closer. 'They'd maybe been there since quite early this morning. Bede, I'm so sorry.'

I'd always been Reger to her before. As if that mattered.

'They've been very good, the people here,' she went on when the security officers were within earshot. 'They're taking care of everything. They just said to leave it all to them.'

On this island Lani had been doing a lot of garden work, which would have brought her into contact with local men.

'She looked completely peaceful, they said.'

'They?' I repeated dully.

'Frick. Frick and a couple of the boys. The ones who were asked to identify her. Peaceful and, of course, so very lovely.'

Sempra had begun to weep. 'Please don't be angry with her, Bede,' she said, pressing her face into my upper arm. 'She'd been so terribly unhappy for such a long time.'

The middle-aged security women looked as if they expected me to present some kind of difficulty. Before turning to go I murmured a few words of gratitude to them: for catering for us not just in life, but also now after it.

'At least thanks to Lani you've got your writing,' said Sempra, when we were back on the proper road. 'It's bound to be a help to you.'

I looked behind me and one of the women was now stooped over, picking up the clothing, while the other was holding open a drum-like receptacle for her to drop it all into. The last item I'd seen on the grass was the black velvet choker with its small silver stud that Lani had called her Adam's Apple.

That evening there was an informal session for members of the group who wanted to share memories of Lani over a drink.

Twenty or so of us took part. Zephyr, whose gravelly voice Lani had especially enjoyed me taking off, said "our precious sister" had passed through a gateway to eternity. All I could think was that Lani and I could no longer send our own little dabs of colour back through the prism which had fused us all.

By then, to comply with directives still in place from the blackout (a printed note told us), both bodies had already been incinerated. Frick, again, was asked to be present for this.

First thing next morning we left the island.

No one suggested we had to be moved on for our own good, but we imagined how it may have looked for an islander to lose his life after mixing with us. And perhaps a few in the cohort resented the way Lani had run the risk of jeopardizing the sometimes delicate relationship with our hosts.

Many of the others spoke to me on the night before our departure. Like Sempra, they were sorry for my personal loss. Like her too, they stressed Lani's deep long-term misery, to the extent that in the end I sensed some general exasperation with me for having failed to persuade her to go on living.

I drank myself to a standstill, half-afraid I might come undocked and go down with all hands. Already I think I'd begun to sense that a death could shape a life over a much longer term, but I said almost nothing. To have admitted that for all her withdrawals, Lani had never seemed to me any less fundamentally positive about living than the rest of us might not have cut much ice.

In the following period, Lani's name was effectively as taboo as that of anyone who ever left to make a new life with an islander. Her absence must have remained active, but we saw ourselves as lucky, smiled-upon. Something like this did not fit the picture.

Before we fetched up at the island still known for security reasons by its blackout name of "O", she was mentioned only once. Someone had spotted an islander who looked like her ('a bit older, shorter hair, much longer skirt'). We were out on the water, and at first the rest of us in the boat only nodded. Then Atman put into words what we all may have been thinking:

'At least we now know that we must be alive!'

This wasn't quite as crass as it sounds.

From the start we'd found the islanders' ideas about us mildly diverting, usually picked up from overheard remarks made by bar staff or block cleaners. But it was Lani who'd come up with the notion that before we formed the cohort we'd all died then passed through to an "afterworld".

People say all sorts of things. (There were islanders who called us "God's Children".) But for a while this notion stuck. We even amused ourselves by acting up in private like zombies.

Atman's comment soon did the rounds. That night in the dorm I bedded down next to Tchure. He watched Atman walk the length of the room away from us, toothbrush in hand, towel slung over his shoulder. Then Tchure turned my way.

'But, my dear boy,' he said with his most dazzling smile from inside his tented-up duvet, 'who says you can't die twice?'

xiv

Sempra must have had her own idea on how "my writing" would help. As it happens, until writing this I've never put anything on paper about Lani. Nor have I ever spoken about her, save during the official hearings, when often I would wonder what responses Lani might've been better-placed to give.

For a long while I wrote nothing at all. And not wanting the others to know I was effectively dropping the baton that Lani had handed me, I took myself off for long periods, as she herself had.

Really all I was doing was waiting. For what, I didn't know.

When I was with the others, I fell in with their grassing-over of the recent past, but alone on shore after shore I would sense myself haemorrhaging out into the huge ocean air with no idea where I stopped and the awful living light began.

I remember one afternoon, as a train rattled past on an elevated railway, feeling as if a roar had formed at the back of my throat, but instead of bursting out of me it had burrowed in deeper, maybe to merge with similar echoing silences.

I could have done with some of Tchure's kicking, jabbing fire-ball energy. After spending two nights away with an islander he now came back waving an old offprint that had been pushed under all his rooming-house's doors. 'Voice of a generation!' he yelled at me, and I smiled at the absurdity, but I admit that at the same time I wondered what richer, more collectively silent voice I might be losing. I had no interest whatever in becoming more "who I was" as an individual. What I'd always most wanted was for all of us, together, to be more "who we were".

And whenever I closed my eyes whilst sitting so ineffectually out on a rocky perch, I would again be back beneath the workbench as the wood came raining down.

I'd sway then where I sat, shut my eyes tighter, gasp at the smell of the sweet musky shavings, the feel of them brushing my face, my uncovered arms. Just in those few moments I would wish with all the fervour in me that I could dredge up different scenes from my own lost past, driving the knife in deeper but only then to wedge it tighter and stop any more of me from seeping out through the great savage gash left by Lani.

And still I don't know if I willed this to happen, but it was around now too that I started to sense – just as Lani may have before me – someone approaching across the water as I sat with the book. Not always, and no one I could yet see. A person I'd perhaps once known. A woman who wasn't Lani.

Rayga, she'd call, then be gone again.

Rayga –

In the end, fixating on that heart-shaped outline made partly out of Lani's garments, I began to fill some pages.

Not much more than five-finger exercises, but from these a single phrase emerged. "French doors." I didn't intend it to. Prompted by Lani's loss, it just came. Over time, a truncated episode floated up through the fog in my mind to accompany it, and it's never left me since.

A leaf-strewn lawn seen through locked French doors. Small smeared panes chipped here, cracked there; a candy-floss of cobwebs streaking the outer glass. A feeling I was being invited not to look out on a breaking day, wherever it was, but to turn away instead and face the knocked-through room that I knew lay behind me, to a woman who'd be there.

Then as I turned, darkness fell again beyond the glass. Yet the thin light still trapped indoors seemed to freshen and gather against the stripped floorboards, the bare walls. It was so much emptier in this room than out there, with less to be illuminated, less for the precious breaking light to wear itself out on.

In my notebooks I kept coming back to this, mainly out of embarrassment at its sheer incompleteness. It seemed that the more often I put myself behind those French doors, the clearer I saw things, the less fragmentary the scene became.

I didn't know where it came from.

For all its insistence, it felt less like something I'd lived through than something still to come – perhaps the future falls open anywhere too – or had I once dreamed it, with gentle marimba music drifting in around me, a confidential whisper, a creak of stairs followed by the harsher clip of heels on hallway parquet? And why did every word I wrote about this seem to come framed by the half-smile of that nameless girl on the funicular railway?

Meanwhile, shortly before we came to the island of "O", I noticed a change within our group, most particularly in the breaking mornings.

For so long it had always been the same way: huge skies above the latest block, scrubby lawns cut through by concrete pathways and crusted mud tracks; our bleary looks and smiles then would be so warm, particularly from the girls, smiles that said, "So we've come this far – now we're all set again".

Times without number I'd seen and given these smiles. They drew up to attention something inside me I could never imagine living without. But after Quaye grinned back at me over her upturned raffia-like coat collar on the morning we left for O, she quickly looked away. Others did too.

I know that after we lost Lani, it was I who had so often gone off alone. But even if there was no sense that I was about to take a step forward, the rest may have already taken a step back.

XV

We had guessed O was a big island even before we were driven in large decommissioned service vehicles through shallow mountains to its farther, more built-up shore.

We'd landed in a cove beneath a rocky promontory where a well-lit oak cabin with a curved copper roof stood on short stilts like a squat sea-facing clock, strong orange light glowing at all its windows, both oblong and circular.

Only the dozen or so truck drivers were there to meet us, but one of our grander (and prompter) reception parties had been organized in a clifftop field not far from the residential block.

I say block, but this was one of those country-house conversions I mentioned earlier, an imposing mansion with caribou heads still in place over the doorways, gilt-framed portraits up the stairs.

They gave us a lot to drink, and little of the evening stayed with me. I can't imagine what made me bring up again to the others the cabin we'd seen back at our landing point. Nor do I remember asking our hosts whose home it was, though in the morning I was assured that I did, repeatedly, and it seems an arrangement was made for me to revisit that quarter soon.

All I now see from that night, more acutely than ever, is everyone else in our party smiling and falling away from me.

I woke up late in an empty dorm, still in my coat and all the rest of my clothes. Just one of our girls, Jenufa, was out in the compound, flicking through a very old dance magazine.

It was she who told me how interested I'd been in the cabin the night before. The lighthouse, she called it.

Most of the others had gone to work, she added, or to look for a bar with sensible opening hours. 'They send you their best,' she said with a smile which made her recede right there on the bench where she sat.

'Your driver is waiting outside.'

The day was fine and still. The man behind the wheel, stripped to the waist, insisted I travel in the "better-sprung" back seat of his car. He said nothing more until we arrived.

I was dropped outside a taverna I hadn't seen the night before, set well back from a walled, semi-circular terrace that led down to the landing stage where our boats now bobbed about in water as clear as zero.

Other buildings were dotted around the crescent-shaped inlet with its thumbnail sandy bay: almost a little village of boxy, flat-roofed white-stone villas with dark blue doors and balcony rails. At the tip of the headland, beyond the oak-plank "lighthouse" that loomed larger by sunlight, stood a ruined fort on a spill of pockmarked volcanic rock.

A waitress with short bleached hair, slightly younger than ourselves, was energetically sluicing the taverna patio's flagstones. Every one of its shaded tables was unoccupied.

'So what'll it be?' she asked with a bright open smile, straightening up as I approached and allowing me to see the name "Ute" on her tag. 'Coffee? Lunch? A room?'

Our eyes met and it seemed to me that her smile raced forward to cover all the ground my own people's had been leaving bare. I don't think I'd been so aware of the sun's strength since the day it first broke properly through on the downland.

'For you, I think,' said Ute, 'it's a room, with no mirror – yes? Full board.'

I can't say I had been expected personally, but the arrival of one of us seemed to have been anticipated. Nothing at all, then or later, was said about payment.

Following Ute indoors, I wondered if that skinny barracks child on the beach, so long ago now, had felt this way as he climbed his stairs of air after crossing the tideline, and although no heart-shaped shaft of light followed me in, I found an immediate new clarity.

Even now I remember with unmatched vividness everything that would unfold before I saw my people again.

There were many less agreeable spots than this inlet to lay up for a period of re-tuning (as I'd sold it to myself). The single room was serviceable, and the "comestibles" came in generous helpings. I could have stayed high from dawn to dusk.

Even in the last moments before arriving by truck or car, the landscape here would look exhausted, leached of life. Then the carefully-cultivated riot of flowers, bushes and palms would rear up "like a dream of forgotten kisses" according to Ute (the youngest of the taverna patron's four grown-up children), mainly bougainvilleas, oleanders, geraniums and purple thyme, she said.

Roughly hacked-out steps led halfway down the terrace to a crazy-paved platform. Ute would sunbathe here while her brothers busied themselves servicing our boats lower down.

As she made her sinewy off-duty dives I'd watch from the spill of rock by the fort which I made my regular writing seat. She told me the water felt heavier than it looked – silky and warm, folding itself around the swimmer as if its surface hadn't really been broken.

I'd look back too at the taverna with its empty tables and blue-and-white striped canvas chairs under canopies. In the silent heat all the pinks, purples, whites and reds, along with the skitterings of lemon butterflies, could distract me for hours.

This was a different order of quiet from anything I'd so far known. A stillness, a sense of being becalmed, which I didn't so much seem to be tapping into as radiating outward.

In many ways I welcomed it. I loved being part of the group, but since starting to write, and especially since losing Lani, I'd felt rather less inclined to jest around for the others. I'd also begun to wonder what else I might have to offer.

Now I didn't have to concern myself with that. I didn't really have to concern myself with anything. In all the time I was there I seldom wrote much, which I also knew didn't matter.

Again, I was not so much writing as waiting.

xvi

Whenever in the past one of our number spent time away from the blocks, I'd always be impressed by their confidence that the rest of us wouldn't just up and leave. But every day on O I had the reassurance of being able to glance across at our boats.

Nor was I completely estranged from the others.

In twos and threes they'd hitch-hike over to sit and sun themselves with me. Twice, early on, Tchure came alone. As happened on some of our longer stays, the lockers here were replenished by night, and once he brought with him some new writing materials which I didn't yet need.

The second time, he was already down on the thumbnail bay when I arrived, as if to clock me on. He'd scratched both my names into the sand in tall capitals. Before he left he shook my hand so hard I temporarily lost the feeling in two fingers.

Later that morning, after managing only to reach the end of a first paragraph, I picked my way back down to the bay.

In my coat I paddled among shoals of small thin fish, with green and white plants fizzing out of the grey rock around me.

'They're capers!' Ute surprised me by calling out from her platform when she saw me fingering them.

She came to stand close by me, barefoot in the tie-dyed shirt-dress she always wore over her wisp of a bikini. She smiled at what Tchure had inscribed on the sand.

'"REGER BEDE,"' she read, raising then lowering her outsized shades, pronouncing both words perfectly, swirling them around in her mouth like two spoonfuls of her father's home-made breakfast honey. 'All those Es, and each with a different sound! Though that last one doesn't really have a sound at all, does it? It just saves you from being "BED".'

I murmured that there were worse things for an E to do and she laughed. Already I'd spent more time with her than with any other islander since the beginning of our journey.

She told me with a grin she had read a number of my "*Heart of Light* leaflets". 'We like how so many of your pieces are nostalgic,' she went on, suddenly becoming serious. 'Full of longing for that moment when everything moves on to the next stage.'

I nodded, without a clue what she meant. She could have been sending me up.

'That room you've described – with the French doors? – it's as if I actually know it. Not all of us can see it. Some people even say it should be French windows! But after a while, for me, it's kind of like my own house. Not this one here now, but back when I was a kid. The old dark things outside, and the turning away to the new things. I'm back in that space again, at the moment it all changed. You really do capture the feeling.'

I thanked her and looked out along the headland, taking in all the empty white villas.

'It's been a while since we've seen anything of yours,' Ute said when next we spoke. 'Maybe you'll find fresh inspiration out here.'

I smiled at her and said yes, maybe.

But such an air of absence hung over this tiny island paradise, with everyone gone. I imagined it in a different season teeming with people. But what sort of a season would that be, when the climate right now could not be bettered?

'All those houses belong to her,' said Ute with a curt nod towards the cabin. 'The woman who lives there. The owner, we call her. The taverna's actually hers too. We're only leasing it. This is her whole little manor!'

She'd mentioned an owner before, and like Jenufa she'd called her cabin a "lighthouse", though that's not what it was nor ever could have been: a structure built specifically to be skirted. Ute went in twice a week to clean. 'It's just a studio really, a studio where she happens to live, her being an artist and all.'

I asked if this owner was the other regular swimmer and Ute nodded.

I'd seen her out in the water, only ever at a distance. A golden-haired back-stroker with a powerful, languid style. Each time she raised an arm and gave a graceful turn to her wrist, I imagined her reaching up to pluck fruit.

Finding Ute easy to talk to, I asked about the wiry, long-backed and sometimes flamboyantly-dressed man who sat watching her swim from the shore, his clasped palms resting on top of a shooting stick. Was he perhaps the owner's father?

'Oh no,' Ute replied, 'her father isn't with us anymore. He was lovely. It was him who built the lighthouse, all ecologically sound and energy efficient! It has to be. You wouldn't believe the winds we get here. Over a hundred miles an hour. Rocks fly!'

She stooped, picked up a pebble and made it skip six times across the water's surface before clapping her hands like an impish child. As I made to leave, she gave me a look up and down.

'You must be so hot in your overcoat,' she said. 'You can take it off here, you know. I wouldn't tell anyone! I wouldn't say a word to your friend.'

'My friend?'

'The one in the frock coat, who smells of very rich fruitcake!'

She meant Tchure. I directed a vague smile past Ute towards the building that now even I was starting to see as a lighthouse, beneath which a small, unusually-shaped wooden boat was tethered to its own private landing stage.

Ute turned to face it too.

'She draws you, the owner,' she said quietly. 'I've seen her. While you sit out there on the rocks writing, she draws you.'

As an artist, there was no reason why she shouldn't. But lying half-awake in bed at nights, retracing the arcs of Ute's dives, I'd hear "she draws you, she draws you" until I saw not a person with charcoal and paper but the silhouette of a woman reeling me in to the lighthouse on the finest of lines, a line too robust for any hundred-mile-an-hour wind ever to snap.

xvii

I never did see her sketching me. But keeping a closer eye on her lighthouse, I several times watched her slam its front door shut, or trot out to her battered four-wheel drive, then kick up great mares' tails of dust as she roared away into the interior.

She looked like a person who did everything economically fast: pulling on clothes, raking a brush through her mane of hair which once I saw tamed into a short, fat plait, wolfing back meals on the hoof behind her strange home's untreated walls that were already starting to silver with age.

She gave off a different sort of energy from Ute, not just because she was ten to fifteen years older. All her movements were smoother, less loud, more sinuous and – I have to say even from my spot on the rocks – sadder. Since our very first islands, I'd seen no one whose heart looked more fingermarked.

The first time we spoke she'd just parked up on her sunken gravel drive. I was passing on the way out to my perch.

Shortly beforehand I'd heard impatiently raised voices. Now I saw the older man Ute hadn't identified letting himself indoors.

The "owner" called hello to me through her opened driver-door window. 'So how are you getting on?' she said.

In all the time I was to know her, almost everything she said would be defiantly ordinary, but her smile came from somewhere else. I saw it even before I took in the decisive features behind it: a more intense version of the smile I'd seen on the face of the girl on the funicular railway. As soon as this smile of hers started, she seemed to check herself and put it into reverse; a smile on its way home from a ripe old laugh.

'I'm Opal,' she said, making no move to unfasten her seatbelt, a tiny smudge of pale green paint near the hinge of her jaw. 'This is my estate. It used to be my father's, now for my sins it's mine!' She made no mention of her art.

'Reger,' I told her, since she seemed to be waiting to be told. 'Reger Bede.'

She nodded. 'And you're travelling?'

Travellers was what Ute and the other, younger, taverna staff called us too, but on this handsome woman's lips the word didn't sound quite so quixotic.

I waved an arm out at the rocks. 'I write,' I said to explain what I did out there, what she drew me doing.

'Well, you're most welcome,' was all she replied, with no smile of any kind now, before abruptly she restarted her engine, causing me to move on out of her path.

Not long afterwards I heard Tchure laughing with Ute up on the crazy-paved platform. I waved from my rocks and they waved back. Neither seemed to be wearing anything but sunglasses.

This turned out to be the beginning of Tchure's daily visits, as those from the others began to fall away.

He'd time them to coincide with breaks in Ute's shifts, but he came over to me before or after, and he got into a routine ("to save you having to bother") of taking back to my locker whatever pages, detached from the book, I had managed to fill that day. In the past I had only ever submitted wholly intact "volumes", and never until the moment just before our departure. It was all the same to me now.

Tchure never commented on what I'd written. He was far from unintelligent but certainly no reader, and though the cohort's consensus was that over time he had begun to mellow, even his reflectiveness was of the crazy cartwheeling kind.

He'd play with words like toys, seizing on regular everyday phrases like "time-consuming" or "what time do you make it?" and take them to preposterously literal extremes.

Like me, though, he was by nature no loner, and he showed some curiosity in what it was like to spend so much time on my own. He seemed also to have developed his views about the keeper of the book being the voice of a generation.

'There's a sense, isn't there,' he said one time, 'that the person who keeps the log is the sort of conscience of the group?'

He'd say things like this while pirouetting on the spot.

'I mean, we hear that some islanders see us as *their* conscience, zeitgeist, spirit of the age or whatever?' As he spoke that day he appeared to be arm-wrestling with himself. 'Well, isn't the one who keeps the log the sort of essence of it all?'

'It isn't actually a log,' I told him back, aware this would go in one ear and out the other. 'Lani was always clear about that.'

The sound of Lani's name briefly had a calming effect.

He widened his eyes at me. 'Ah, Lani, lovely Lani! I had my chance there but I was only ever keeping her warm for you, dear boy, you know that. Frick. Me. All of us were. Bede's the man. A man apart!' Then he grimaced. 'But sometimes I do wonder – if Lani had kept on writing, d'you think she might still be with us?'

There was nothing like accusation in Tchure's voice, but before this I had wondered if there might be some suspicion I had muscled the book out of her hands, and if that was so, then the others hadn't exactly cast me out, just set me set slightly adrift for a while, with the equivalent of a hammer-shaped tool for beating off larger seabirds. It was hard, too, to know if Tchure kept coming to talk to me purely off his own bat or as a mouth-piece for the group.

But I knew I'd not get a straight answer to that even if I asked him. Already he'd returned to his strenuous callisthenics.

'You really are a bit like the spirit of the age, Bede,' he said with a chuckle. 'You stand alone, a nonpareil! Our own rather marvellous zeitgeist!'

94

He nodded at my blank page.

'You're the one who comes to wind our clocks.'

He also teased me about the owner, saying Ute had seen snap-shots of me pinned up in "that lighthouse of hers" – "moody monochrome studies, telephoto lens for the closer facial detail!"

What Ute said was true: Tchure's sweat did smell richly of fruit steeped in spirits. I wondered if he'd confused Opal's sketches of me with photographs. I hoped in a way that he had.

Photos, for all of us, still signified an end, a pulling-out of the group and a putting-down of new roots – and I couldn't imagine anyone doing that here. The whole place had such a left-behind air, as if almost everyone had long since departed and everything was now slowly, irresistibly closing down.

I picked this up even from Opal: the way she'd said "the estate" had once been her father's; the brisk, brave manner of a woman men moved on from. But then, not entirely unexpectedly, Opal made a move towards me.

xviii

Ute came to my room to deliver a note in an unsealed envelope: an invitation for an evening drink.

'Just a drink,' Opal made clear in a sharply sloping hand. 'There's something you might like to see.'

Ute told me something else in a small voice from the doorway. 'Tchure and I – we're getting engaged,' she said. 'My parents are giving us a party. For all your people and all mine. Outside in the open. An engagement party!'

She threw up a hand, splay-fingered, as if to show she was holding nothing threatening. 'We're going to have rings!'

Her eyes glistened as I told her how glad I was.

And I meant what I said, but not just on her account. Since only one couple ever formed per island, whatever might now be about to happen between Opal and me (and something surely had to happen, or why else had the others eased me into her little domain?), the hybrid couple here had to be Ute and Tchure.

Opal must have spotted me on my way over from the taverna.

After climbing the narrow wooden steps to the lighthouse, I found she had left its front door ajar. She called out to me above the drumming of a shower, telling me to come in, make myself at home, feel free to pour a drink.

Ute had been at work inside. Stripped pine floorboards shimmered spotlessly right across the big, airy, double-height space that made up the open-plan kitchen, sitting-out and dining areas. There was a great deal of chrome, several futons with plumped-up pastel cushions. A pine ladder led up to a mezzanine floor for sleeping while directly below was the closed blue door to the bathroom.

The seaward wall was made entirely of glass. One of the picture windows had been slid open so I went through to the slatted balcony where a bottle of wine sat chilling in a bucket with a pair of long-stemmed glasses also nestling in the ice.

I took the nearer canvas chair and waited, watching the sea.

Opal took an age to appear. The evening sun was setting directly ahead, sliding fast into the tranquil water. With sea on three sides, I could actually have been out on one of our boats, and I did feel at home – home from home – as I worked my way through half the wine, playing with Lani's pebble in my coat pocket.

I'd guessed I was there to see Opal's picture of me. She might even have intended me to nose it out for myself – canvases stood stacked everywhere, with more work on the walls. Most were little more than washes of watery colour, some with long thin strands of darker paint running across them like taut strings on a musical instrument.

At last I heard the bathroom door open and caught a scent of drenched grass as Opal padded out to me.

'Here,' she smiled, extending her arm when I stood and turned to face her. 'Let me take your coat.'

She put on a cassette of choral music, then came back with olives and a second bottle. Sitting with her legs tucked beneath her, she plucked at her ankle-length dress to stop it from stretching. Droplets from her wet hair sat on her bare shoulders like the beads of condensation on both the bottles we emptied.

With the choral anthems on repeat-play and made bolder by my talks with Ute, I asked Opal if she'd always been an artist.

She laughed. 'I'd hesitate to call myself that. I haven't always even wanted to be one.'

'What else did you want to be?'

'Oh!' She laughed again, fondly now, then her smile became inward. 'A spy, perhaps?'

'This would have been before the blackout?'

'The what?'

There was a whole other world in her open, friendly, puzzled expression; a world as yet undiscovered by me.

I shook my head and smiled.

After that, there was no more talk of "before". No talk at all about what had led us to this balcony, on this night, sitting under a clouded moon still new enough to wish on; only about the fierce island storms, the celebrated local varieties of butterfly, the new independent radio station. In later years I'd find that some people's small talk flows toward something larger, while with others it flows purposefully away. Opal's just pooled: deeper, clearer.

'You wanted me to see something?' I asked since this seemed to have slipped her mind, and I was interested to see how I might look as a marbled abstract of greys and greens, a quiverful of threads.

I caught that strange stifled smile of hers again: a genie just failing to push the cork up out of its bottle. It was as if she'd got wind of one of our cohort's lewdest running jokes, one she shouldn't have begun to understand, let alone find funny.

She gestured beyond her balcony. 'Only this really. The sunset. They're so spectacular from this spot.'

I told her it had been wonderful, though in truth I'd scarcely noticed it. 'Everything's wonderful here,' I added.

Our eyes met. She nodded, waiting and not waiting. *So this is me*, her gentle, level look seemed to be saying.

'I hear you've been drawing me,' I said. 'Was it for a painting?'

'Oh.' Her eyes stayed on mine. 'That's a work in progress.'

We both fell silent, but I didn't want to leave quite yet. She attracted me. I could imagine staying on until the new sun rose, the choral singers' slow sad harmonies coiling up around us.

'Will you come over again?' she asked finally, focusing on a point way out to sea. From her neutral tone she might have been asking me the time, or even what time I made it.

I told her I'd have to, if I was ever going to see my picture.

'"Your" picture?'

'The work in progress.'

Still her head was turned away from me.

'You may not like it. I'm not sure I do.'

She saw me to her door, helped me back on with my coat.

'The weather isn't always this agreeable,' she said before sending me off with a studied touch to my arm. 'You're welcome to spend time here during the day, if that would suit you.'

xix

I'd have gone back anyway, but disruptions in and around the taverna sent me sooner, then frequently.

Carloads of Ute's young friends were turning up ahead of her big party, bedding down at night in a new marquee, spilling out over the rocks to smoke and drink by day.

There was no change in the weather, so the half-dozen times I visited the lighthouse I'd scratch out my few words sitting on the balcony, which as Opal had indicated could be accessed by an external flight of steps even when she was away.

At the foot of these steps was the door to what she called "a bolthole, with facilities", which she told me she would leave unlocked for my use. It turned out to be a small but beautifully-appointed self-contained flat with a wide sea-facing window.

The picture windows upstairs stayed locked, though.

She'd use the external steps when she came to pass time with me, usually bringing a coffee percolator with mugs, never enquiring about my writing, never mentioning her own work.

Once from the balcony I heard raised voices again deep inside, another time the distant low grunts and lighter rhythmic sighing of two lovers. But soon afterwards another argument sparked, and as a door banged shut I heard Opal call out tearfully, 'This was never, ever, what I wanted – '

Tchure soon deduced where I'd be and would wait near Opal's steps for me to hand over my pages.

He'd be pleased if I gave him a healthy number. There were rarely now messages from the others. One afternoon he produced a pack of contraceptive sheaths, "from the locker".

'My locker?' I asked.

'Purely discretionary.' He winked, this eternal stranger to discretion himself, as he slipped them back into his pocket. 'Far be it from me to come between you and F.R.I!'

But he did leave me that day with a brand new notebook, the same shape and style as all the others, though maybe twice as fat.

Tchure seemed to spend most of his own time in the little plastic-and-fabric party city that had sprung up around the taverna prior to his engagement party (or "engorgement event" as it never stopped delighting him to call it).

Before the boats left each island, no couple had to specify whether they'd be coming on with us or staying behind. But everything Tchure said to me suggested he would not be able to leave this place; and Ute had such close ties with her family and friends, I couldn't imagine her wanting to sever them.

It's hard to say how, as a group, we ever decided it was time to leave. Island by island, a consensus must have been reached, much as it was about a person's name.

Maybe one of the natural leaders, a Zhiyin or Frick, subtly made a call, behind which the rest of us then fell in. All I remember now is heading sleepy-eyed to each dawn quayside and knowing in my bones that this was the place I was required to be.

On O, my hunch was that we'd all be moving on after Ute and Tchure's event. This was, after all, the place where we'd arrived, and soon everyone would be coming back to it. After partying through the night, we'd surely head straight out.

The day before, as I was leaving the lighthouse where I had been dozing on the bolthole's double bed for a couple of hours, Opal drew up on her drive and called out to me to come back later for a crayfish barbecue. I didn't realize I would be her only guest.

We ate on the balcony. She hadn't changed out of her paint-smeared smock but had carefully drawn back and plaited her hair, accentuating her clear skin and good cheekbones.

This time we reached a third bottle of her tart white wine, half way through which I said it seemed an age since I'd last seen all the others.

She smiled, never having asked a thing about them – us – and there were times, even then, when I was unsure if she knew who we "travellers" were. (The first time we talked I referred to them as "my people", and she gave me a glance of what looked like the purest compassion.)

When I asked what she made of Tchure, again she just smiled, not enigmatically, more as if she did not understand the question, or had long ago stopped making that sort of assessment. But she did open up a little about her work and through that, without perhaps meaning to, about herself.

XX

The canvases on show in the main room, she explained, weren't hers but the work of students – "urchins!" – some of whom she still went off to teach even though she was supposed to be on sabbatical. The bulk of her earned income, she made clear, came not from exhibiting or selling her own work but from teaching.

'I don't really "do",' she admitted. 'I don't suppose I've ever really had it – whatever it is one has to have.'

But I persuaded her to show me some of her water-colours, which turned out to be in much the same style as all the rest. Greys sometimes rising to purples, mostly washes of grey into pale green: marbled abstracts, qualities of light, their atmospheres ranging from resignation to bereftness. And though I'd thought the threads that ran across the other pictures looked like smooth harp strings, I saw tiny pointed clusters at intervals along her own, a little like barbed wire.

Only one painting was titled – a virtually blank grey canvas called "Tying the Knot". I asked if this was intended to be an engagement present for the happy couple.

Opal shook her head. 'I've already given them something else. One they asked for, as a matter of fact. I can't think why – it didn't really work.' She darted her bottled smile at me, the genie all but breaking free. 'It was my portrait of you.'

I'd stopped asking her about that piece.

This, for me, was conclusive proof that Tchure and Ute were planning to stay on the island. Opal didn't paint small. One of her hefty six-foot canvases was never going to fit into a boat.

She touched the corner of "Tying the Knot", gingerly, as if contact might spark a shock. She may have been drawing to my attention that under its title were the fainter words, "For Parr".

'No,' she said, 'this picture is much older. Another world.'

Another and better world, I was meant to understand from the way she said it, and I imagined who Parr must be, but she offered no further explanation.

This was our trick: we'd started from scratch then stayed at scratch. It was as if we had both spent all our lives storing things up that we were never going to tell each other.

If this grey wash marked the tying of some old knot of her own, a knot long since unpicked or slashed to bits, it was sad, but not for me to share. Yet even in our few times together I had noted an aura of loss building up around her. She seemed to breathe it out. It made me think of those unoccupied villas Ute had called "the owner's little manor" – not ready and waiting for holidaymakers to move into, but perennially empty reminders of what had been and gone, just there to underline Opal's isolation.

We were still looking at the picture when Opal's phone rang.

She glanced at her watch before picking up the handset. The incoming call, about a student who'd got into difficulties, was one she told me apologetically she would have to take. But when I made to duck out, she put a hand to my chest and shook her head.

It wasn't a short conversation.

Opal had to sit at her desk, put on reading glasses and consult paperwork while she talked. Without looking up, she asked if I'd bring across a manila folder from a nearby low table. In taking it, her hand brushed mine.

She motioned for me to stay. Then, continuing to answer her colleague's questions, she reached for my hand and placed it on her bowed neck under the plait, as if asking for a blessing.

As she spoke she rolled her shoulders under my touch, which I took as encouragement to stroke her satin skin, and before she was done I'd not only run my palm around her throat to the dip between her prominent collarbones, I had slid my hand down inside her loose smock to cup the swell of her breast, at which point she shifted her free arm to pin me closer.

When she stood to disengage herself, I saw a spot of new colour high on either cheek.

'I'm sorry,' she said. 'But I can't. Not yet.'

She looked away, seeming for a moment to teeter on her feet. 'There's something I'm still coming out of.'

Then she pressed a fingertip into a shirt button near my breastbone, and used it as if to spring backwards.

'But I'm not playing with you,' she said. 'I wouldn't do that.'

Before returning to the taverna I said how indebted to her I was for all the hospitality she'd shown me. With a smile she went up on her toes to kiss me beside my mouth.

I had no reason to believe she'd bother with the party; neither of us had mentioned it, and she didn't seem to fit into any kind of company. Our moment appeared to have come and gone. After saying goodbye that evening, I didn't expect we would see each other again.

xxi

I spent the last day of our stay on the island exploring the hinterland to this spot I had made my home from home.

I'd hoped that away from the coast my pen might move less sluggishly across the new notebook's pages but I didn't even make a mark. Looking forward to re-joining the group made it hard to concentrate on anything else.

I returned at dusk to find large numbers of Ute's friends and relatives already drinking at outside tables. Some had started dancing to calypsos played by a local band dressed in lemon-yellow shirts.

The guests' lavish jewellery and smart-casual outfits made me feel too conspicuous in my old coat to join in at once. So I watched the party's early stages from my narrow balcony, working my way through a complimentary bottle of the potent local rum from the bar, with one eye on the road for the trucks that would be ferrying everyone across from our block.

And in the end, they came.

Cheers went up as those down below swarmed towards the parking bay, firing off corks from bottles of carbonated wine.

The convoy's headlights swept into view just as Opal appeared. It was as if she'd picked the perfect moment for her own arrival to go unnoticed by everyone but me.

I'd never seen her in heels: smart, black, open-toed court shoes. She wore a knee-length, short-sleeved green and black print dress that buttoned down the front. Her tumbling hair looked much glossier than usual too, its natural gold accentuated by rouge on her cheeks, and a savage slash of lipstick making her arms and legs look intensely bare under all the artificial light. There was no sign of her older man.

She stood looking up at me, hands on hips, a pair of chunky bangles on her left forearm. Tilting her head, she asked with her eyes if she should come up. But my own eyes were drawn away to the people being helped down from the trucks.

Riace, Dasein, Balqis, Ren, Kintsugi, Zephyr – my brothers and my sisters, all present and correct, but it wasn't them as individuals I was seeing, just the collection of hand-me-down ball gowns and dinner jackets they all wore.

When I looked directly below again Opal had gone. In her place stood Tchure, also black-tied in a jacket several sizes too large for him. A dark leather thong circled his neck and a glinting silver ring was threaded onto it. 'Can't get it on my finger!' he yelled up at me above the music, yanking at it like a miniature noose.

'Need to get it adjusted.'

'Is there a penguin suit for me?' I yelled back.

He shrugged. 'All these stupid outfits were in our lockers.' Then he was called away without saying where mine was.

'There's a tuxedo back in my wardrobe that would probably fit you,' said a voice from my room's doorway. 'Shall I fetch it?'

In the heels Opal was almost able to look me in the eye. Again both her hands were on her hips as if she was squaring up to me, and she did cut an impressive figure: a woman in every detail, where our girls looked as if they'd raided a fancy-dress box. Even her expression had a sleek new edge to it.

But I told her not to bother and came away from the window. Lurched might be the better word. It wasn't just the rum. Already unsure what was happening, I didn't want to hear what would fit me – not from Opal.

'Well, at least take off your coat,' she said with her quiet smile, reaching out possibly to steady me, but she then let her fingertips rest on my arm.

As carefully as I could, I lifted off her hand, turned it – on an impulse kissed its palm – and asked her to go on down.

She went, but the citrus perfume from her wrist stayed behind. Minutes later, back at the window, I saw her take a chair at one of the smaller tables, adjust her dress after crossing her legs, then begin to run a finger slowly up and down the stem of a flute glass.

I locked my door and lay face down on the bed. From the window I had only just managed to make out my own people's faces, even though I'd been able to count how many buttons above her dress's hemline the seated Opal had left undone.

I couldn't move.

All I had to do was wait. That's how I was reasoning with myself before I lost consciousness. In the morning we'd be gone.

Too much time passed. ("What sort of time d'you call this!") On waking, my pillow was soaked. Clouds of loudness drifted in through the opened window, loaded with swirls of barbecue and dope smoke.

The calypsos had given way to waltzes from a small string orchestra. Again I zoned out and the next time I looked, one of my offprints had been pushed underneath the door.

Only it wasn't one of mine.

Kneeling on the floor to flick through it, I found the odd familiar phrase, but its running heads were *Lighterman*, *Lighterman* to the left, *Tchure* to the right, and in three or four places I saw my own name embedded in the body of the text.

I don't remember getting to the foot of the stairs through the crush of all the bodies. No faces were clear in the smoky press below save that of Tchure himself.

Unable to speak, I handed him his offprint as if it was a ticket of admission, and with his fruitcake bouquet and the ring around his neck he guided me by my coat sleeve through to the packed inner restaurant where several tables had been pushed together to display the couple's engagement gifts.

A group of islander guests, jammed shoulder to shoulder, was admiring a large framed painting propped up on three chairs.

I recognized Opal's signature grey-wash style before I saw this one wasn't just an abstract. Here, the finely-graded range of greys merged to form distinct shapes and shadows. It was like seeing coastal rock in muted sunlight, rock that on closer inspection had been weathered into a face.

My shoulders flamed up inside my coat.

Tchure had gone. No one in here was wearing a black tie or ball gown. Where were all my people? Those nearest were glancing from the painting to me then back at the painting, and looking pleased with themselves for having made the connection.

My hand flew to my chin, my cheeks. Of course I still had my beard but the face in the painting was clean-shaven.

My hand, both hands, patted the hairless parts of my face the way a man pats his jacket for a set of keys. I'd lost track of more than keys. The person in the picture – so beautifully gently rendered – was years older than I'd ever imagined myself to be.

Years. As many as Opal had on Ute, even more.

Involved as I was at its epicentre, the ugliness kicked in fast.

I'd taken Lani's pebble out of my pocket to hold its coolness to my temple. But an islander, assuming I was about to vandalize the portrait, tried to wrench it away from me.

When I resisted, in that tightest of spaces others threw their arms around me and began to force me down.

I used to know this! roiled through my head with flashed-up images of French doors, fluctuating light. I'd lost my place, dispersed between the twin tides of past and future, but only the time to come could now reach back to sweep me on.

The more violently I thrashed, the more restraint I felt on every side. There was laughter all round too, the way I myself had once laughed so helplessly when the blond wooden feathers rained down, but now the voices multiplied: twenty, thirty.

And as the light dimmed, and the harder it became to flail, I realized from the shouts and cries that they thought they were saving me, stopping me from harming myself.

They got me to the floor, their hands not just aiming to restrain me now but to rip away my second skin. First they pulled down my coat around my arms like a straitjacket, then turning me they tore it in a scream from my back.

Before my own new blackout descended, the last word I heard as they twisted me around to face the camera's huge heart-shaped flash, was "Smile!"

xxii

Whoever hauled me over from the taverna didn't just dump me at the foot of the lighthouse's outside steps.

In frosted morning light I woke up on the floor of Opal's dining area. Her green print dress fluttered from a wire hanger hooked over the bathroom door-handle, her heeled shoes lined up neatly underneath.

Warily I got to my feet. With the picture window open, it should have been possible to hear the soft squeak and scrape of our boats being jostled by the rising tide. Shoeless, I stepped out on to the balcony in my stained shirt and jeans.

The light wasn't right: this light barely held back the earlier darkness, which still seemed to be hammering at its underside.

It hurt my ears rather than my eyes, making me feel as if my head had been skewered. Down at the water's edge a solitary man played with his dog, and from somewhere so far away that it may just have been a dream not yet fully faded, I heard small children chanting.

There were no boats.

The party debris reached for some distance along the headland. On my way to the taverna I saw countless bottles, paper plates, wind-blown bunting, a slick of oyster-like condoms, some scraps of discarded clothing around a bouncy castle.

There was just one black bow tie – pre-knotted and fixed to a loop of white elastic which gave it a semi x-rayed look. And there were no boats. No pinnaces.

I didn't see another soul until a blonde waitress came out with a bucket of water to sluice wine spill from the flagstones.

'Ute?' I called, starting to follow the curved terrace wall.

She didn't look up. It wasn't her name.

'Ute's gone,' the waitress explained as if to a child when I passed. 'She went with the travellers in the boats.'

The empty inner restaurant had been scoured clean, all the tables and chairs were back in their usual positions.

Opal's portrait stood on the floor near the exit to the washrooms, half obscured by the drape of my slightly shredded coat. Stapled to its right-hand pocket, the one in which for so long I'd kept Lani's pebble, was a photo in its white-card frame.

So this is you.

Unexpectedly it showed me in profile.

A blind, startled rictus that could have been mistaken for a smile. Bearded, but otherwise indistinguishable from Opal's grey rocky left-facing wash, truly as old as she had made me look, and no longer of the party.

On easing the coat away from the painting, I felt a heaviness that had to be the pebble, still in its proper place. I tore off the photo and threw it down. There was nothing to fetch from my room upstairs. I'd always travelled light. We all had.

With my coat slung over my arm I walked back past the place where the boats weren't.

I tried not to think, but what came to mind was one of the many dinnertime debates we used to have, when we'd drink ourselves senseless and try quite seriously to pool ideas on how to build an even better world. "Once you board the wrong train," Prester C had warned us that particular evening, "every station is the wrong station."

Opal was standing on the lighthouse drive, barefoot in an ivory kimono, watching seabirds wheel high inland. She touched my shoulder as I passed on my way to the bolthole under the balcony: a head-skewered man closing in on middle age, carrying some property retrieved from the scene of an evening he'd prefer to forget, coming home.

I stretched out on the double bed. Whenever I was here, I left the door ajar. It was, after all, Opal's house.

From the bed I watched her ease the door further open. She looked across at me and asked if I needed anything.

Already I could imagine her undemonstratively loosening the sash at her waist before hanging her kimono from the hook on the back of the door. I think I'd started imagining this as soon as I began to use the bolthole, and wanting to see it too.

I thanked her but said no, right at that moment I felt depleted and really just needed more sleep. (The word "depleted" was accurate. The struggle at the taverna had taken a heavier toll than I thought. More than just my coat had been ripped away, and now I had lost my share of our strength in numbers too.)

With an understanding nod Opal stepped back.

My last thought before going under was one of surprise at how the closing of a door can make a room seem much bigger.

3

xxiii

When our residential block on O had been a private mansion, horse-drawn passengers could approach its imposing facade only by following a long curved track.

During this approach, through an artful combination of the land's natural contours with carefully-positioned trees, the great house stayed hidden from view until suddenly – at the completion of the curve – it stood revealed in all its glory.

Thus Voormann Park, as it used to be known, turned out to be the passengers' only possible destination. On alighting, they'd have felt a sense of inevitability about arriving, even though until that last moment they'd have been in the dark about precisely what lay ahead. Just around the bend, so to speak.

To mark a similar sense of inescapability (and maybe even to suggest some familiarity with our new surroundings), we used to say when we reached each new stopover, "So this is us".

So this is me, I might now have said on O. I'd had no idea this phase of my life was about to begin, but as soon as it did, O seemed the only place I could be. And it wasn't just Opal who felt prefigured; the fact that I should enter into her orbit did too. Yet just as the transition we all once made from darkness into laughter had taken time, so now Opal and I did not fall into each other's arms overnight.

xxiv

If as a cohort we spent lifetimes travelling in the boats, my stay on O would have to be measured in eternities, the first of them inside that room made available to me in Opal's lighthouse.

Whatever names for my depletion were suggested by different clinicians, the journey back to health involved little more than bedrest, and a great deal of consideration and generosity from those who attended to me – mainly Opal herself, but also a series of live-in maid-cum-secretaries from the outer housing projects who helped to keep her own increasingly demanding show on the road.

My people were gone and would never stop being gone. There was never a dawn when they didn't seem to have just left.

From my convalescent's bed I was able to look out at the lilac skies and dreaming sea, but with eyes fixed to the horizon I would think of my cohort *as* the sea, with me now so bone dry.

I can't say how long it took for Opal finally to emerge from her relationship with Parr. There's a strong case that she didn't. We were never formally introduced, and I would be a good deal older before I even heard her speak his name.

But during my recovery I grew aware of his intermittent presence, usually marked by the appearance at the mooring place below the terrace of an oddly customized rowboat I had seen before: a kind of floating kennel, with scarcely enough space inside for its rower to sit.

There weren't as many fights as there used to be.

Several times, unseen from my window seat, I saw the pair of them arrive at the lighthouse or drive off together in Opal's latest four-wheel drive, always apparently companionably. The last time would've been well within nine months of the birth of the twins.

When Opal was advised I was ready she took me, in the same four-wheel drive, for what amounted to tours of inspection of the now scarcely-recognizable O.

Great tracts of nearby scrubland had been built over, arrow-straight new highways having opened up its remoter corners. A heliport and then a small airport had appeared, medium-rise condo towers. The rate at which the wider world regrew itself has long been a matter of general record, and in my stupefaction at the sheer scale and intricacy of it all I was far from alone.

Opal could become quite animated in talking me through the many changes. While in full flow she'd dart glances my way, not quite with pride or approval, but almost as if there'd been a kind of trade-off between my depletion and O's flowering, so that any sense of pride or approval should actually be mine.

Closer to home, every bay and inlet to both sides of our headland had fizzed into life as short-stay resorts. Environmentally-minded families colonized Opal's once-desolate estate, and two couples in partnership took over the taverna when Ute's family left.

I asked Opal where they'd gone and she couldn't say.

'They weren't here for long,' she told me in the patient, semi-incredulous way she discussed any subject of no interest to herself. 'Just a year or so. They were never long-term.'

Another time I went so far as to ask – or rather let myself wonder out loud – if O had also been like this in the past.

'So busy everywhere?' I added when she threw me a questioning look. 'Did it used to be like this before?'

'Before?' she repeated, her bright non-plussed smile dissuading me from ever again asking anything similar.

In those earlier years, and later too, even our briefest chats could remind me of a sideshow at the nearby carnival site where the challenge was to pass a small electrified wire hoop along a twisted length of metal – touch it and you set off an alarm.

But I'd never expected talking to lie at the heart of the accord between Opal and me. There was also the matter of not breaking the spell. Because this was a spell. All of it really was magical. A different kind of magic from the cohort's. Ours now.

XXV

Just once, at my request, Opal drove across to the building I still thought of as our residential block.

Now inaccessible behind tall electric fencing, it was undergoing long-term conservation by teams of heritage officers who planned eventually to open it up to the public. Many local people called it not Voormann Park but "The Lawyers' House", on account of complex litigation in an earlier century which had stopped anyone from living inside it for decades.

I'd slept in it as a block just once, on our first drunken night, then never gone back. But I remembered it standing high above the sea, not at the head of a rolling valley.

The whole of O was far bigger than I'd realized. Once I was back to full fitness, after putting in a day's shift at whatever beer-money job I was currently holding down, I'd regularly run through the nights, but still I never reached its further shore.

Locals referred to it not as an island at all but as Hythe prefecture. Apparently they always had, although for the whole of my own stay I would only ever be able to think of it as O.

On that solitary trip to the block, after Opal got me up to speed on Voormann Park's history, we sat looking through the fencing in silence, her hand on my thigh, my hand holding it there.

Before she drove on I think we kissed – we often did – but neither then nor at any other point did she mention my cohort.

As with her silence over Parr, it never struck me that she was being evasive. She surely must've broached certain "ground rules" with me straight after the others all left. Perhaps if you haven't been ready for the start of a conversation, it can get too late to ask for a recap. You never quite catch up.

But I had no reason to want for anything different. Not then. And besides, no one else spoke of Parr either.

Or of my people.

In all my time on O, not one word was ever said about us, nothing written. When visitors were finally admitted to Voormann Park, no reference to our using it as a residential block was made in any of the giftshop literature. Occasional cryptic comments apart, it was as if as a group we didn't exist.

Only for the twins, much later, would this not be the case.

With some of the incomers, once I got out and about, I'd feel on safer conversational ground, at least to pass the time of day.

For them, I could have been living on O since time immemorial: Reger Bede, the night runner from the home of the slightly distant painter lady who always had her business head on when it came to re-negotiating a lease; the guy whose "rock man" portrait hung as if presidentially next to the taverna's vast wall-mounted TV; and not just there either – smaller tourist-board-endorsed prints decorated the walls of shops and bars all over the region.

Sometimes after sundown silent groups of still newer arrivals would sit on the curved terrace under the tamarisks. Another knot might be up on the crazy-paved platform Ute used to dive from.

They'd all watch the silky warm water, quietly encouraging their children to do likewise. There was nothing to see. Not any more. But they all kept their eyes on where our boats once were.

If I paused as I passed them, one or other of the slender tanned women was sure to notice. They'd look up and smile, and when I nodded, their smiles broadened, as if I had validated the reason for their vigil.

I shrank from asking them what they saw in their own minds' eyes, not yet daring to move on from the equivalent of swapping lines from songs or poems. (Except with the twins, I never really moved past that point on O at all. No one else appeared to expect or require it. I almost seemed to spoil my own effect if I spoke.)

On my night runs I'd pound a slow arc around the landscaped grounds where Voormann Park stood and see different clusters camped out there like pilgrims drawn to the source of whatever fading power attracted them: as close to it beyond the high fencing as they, like me, were ever now likely to get.

xxvi

We loved each other, Opal and I. We said so and we meant it. We then advanced from love to sex. I believe it was in that order.

In bed she could seem shocked by her own vigour, which was more than matched in time by my own. It wasn't like a contest between us, exactly; we'd apply ourselves, rather, as if we had already, long before, done something to each other that could only be put right by ever deeper penetration. This was just one of the ways my fetching up with Opal felt foreshadowed.

Most often we'd make love in her bedroom at the lighthouse's higher level, or more urgently still against the glass wall on her balcony. She'd also come down to me in the bolthole.

The whole building was hers, but it seemed important to her that I retain my own space. 'You're really under no obligation to me!' she'd insist with her trademark swallowed smile; and when I signed up for job after job – on the lobster boats, as a breakfast cook, training then serving as a lifeguard – she'd smile the same way, touched that I wanted to make my own meagre contribution to household expenses.

'You don't have to "do",' she'd say in her mild, level way, beaming up briefly from her book. 'Just "be"!'

I disagreed, but nonetheless ended up spending more time as a volunteer than in paid work, mainly visiting the elderly or housebound, getting their shopping in, playing endless games of dominoes for matchsticks. Most of what little I earned, I spent on presents for Opal. Balcony shrubs. Paperbacks about painters or sculptors whose work seemed to have affinities with her own. Chamber music that now came recorded on digital discs.

She received my gifts graciously, while repeating that none was expected. 'All I want is for you to be happy,' was another of her mantras. A mantra – like some of the names we took for ourselves in the cohort – being more about sound than meaning.

I heard there an air of stipulation too. Being happy, staying happy: ultimately this had to be my lookout, just as any decent self-respecting person has to keep his own teeth and hair clean.

Opal spent most of her non-teaching hours in her studio. While she painted she'd often have one of a number of chronologically-ordered family photo albums open nearby. 'Not to work from,' she told me, needlessly, since her ever-denser thread canvases remained defiantly abstract.

Some looked half-way to becoming pure dark blocks but they never went quite that far. Whenever a blackout threatened, I'd look again a few weeks later and she'd have painted out a large number of the threads. "Unravelling!" she called it.

For years the studio doubled as a teaching space for bussed-in groups of teenagers from O's outlying tenement districts. For life-drawing classes Opal used a rota of local models to pose naked, and if a model let her down she'd ask me to sit in.

This was an education for me too.

She got her students to draw with great precision what they could see, not what they assumed must be there, inviting them to start each charcoal sketch by drawing a "negative space", like the heart-shaped gap formed between my arm bent at the elbow and the side of my torso. These were apparently easier to see and draw in proportion than over-familiar body shapes. 'Negative spaces are good,' Opal would say in her calm, affirmative way.

'Shadows like to meet each other,' she'd say too, and I'd find in the waste bin afterwards that she had shown what she meant by conjuring a perfect shoulder, hatching on a scrap of sugar-paper the different levels of shadow cast by my musculature. She was very good indeed at what she did.

Shortly before the twins were born, these classes were discontinued. ("Too much petty pilferage!") The teenagers' attention spans had varied. Some looked too undernourished to concentrate, dressed in clothes so threadbare that I often let them take what they wanted from the pile of my own discarded garments.

That didn't stop them making cracks behind their hands. 'What did they find so funny today?' Opal asked after one session, while slipping off her underwear to join me, at my suggestion, on the divan.

I hesitated, then said what I'd heard from one of the young women: 'All present and correct. He's all present and correct.'

Opal smiled at me as if I'd been speaking backwards.

xxvii

Her sabbatical now behind her, she also commuted between far-flung schools and colleges to teach her urchins, sometimes staying away for weeks on end when exams had to be invigilated.

She never talked about this outreach work. Naturally it crossed my mind that she might be going into barracks schools, but when I referred to them once by that name she just blinked, perplexed. My little metal hoop had nicked the wire. All I could do was blink back, as if I didn't understand myself either.

For as long as I lived on O, I never heard a word about barracks schools. I can't say how many other post-blackout initiatives, if that's what barracks schools were, failed to survive the regrowth.

When Opal was away, alone in the bolthole I'd drink much harder. From the top of the bottle to the bottom of the glass.

Some mornings I'd wake up in my old coat, curled foetus-like around Lani's pebble, which before passing out I must've positioned in the dead centre of what I regarded as Opal's side of the bed – not directly on the under-sheet but on my last, forbiddingly thick, locker notebook, its pages all still blank since I had not continued writing. An amputated hand can't hold a pen, and besides, I had nowhere to leave any pages.

One of these mornings ran on into mid-afternoon.

I didn't know Opal was home until I felt her lips graze my temple. When I turned to greet her, I had to peel the coat's scratchy upturned collar away from my cheekbone.

'Did you get cold?' Opal asked softly, as she perched still in her own jacket next to me on the bed, next to the pebble.

'That's a pretty paperweight,' she said, running her forefinger around both pebble and book without touching either, as if they gave off heat. Then she drifted the back of her hand across my hair, several times, before letting it brush the shoulder of my travel-worn coat, which I admit must have looked alarming: balding to a shine in some places, frayed and darned in others.

'Would you like me to get this cleaned, my love?' she asked.

I couldn't say no, even though it would mean losing every priceless smell that had ever been printed into it.

'Thank you,' I told this kind woman, rising. 'I missed you.'

She'd have been five months pregnant before I realized.

There was no outward show. And I didn't even suspect when fairly abruptly she cut out all smoking and drinking.

All she did was lean against her balcony rail one evening, the waves gushing right in beneath us, and circle a palm over her belly while nodding her head at me.

Tears glistened in her eyes and she looked so alert, so excited. This is how it was with her. She wasn't guarded or secretive, and certainly not without fire or drives. (She wrecked household taps by turning them off too forcefully.)

'I'd thought I might have left it too late – ' she said when I went to kiss her. 'It's twins,' she told me with a wavering smile.

She gave me no time to ask who'd fathered them.

Maybe she saw the question in my eyes, though I don't think it was ever in my heart. She took my hands in hers.

'I can't be sure,' she told me, tears spilling. 'Say now if you need to know.' But without taking a breath she went on, 'I'd so love you to be involved, if you should want that too. There's so much they could take from you! You'd be a fantastic resource!'

She could've said the same to Parr. She maybe already had.

My own eyes brimming, I couldn't have spoken anyway.

It's all out there already, Lani had said, *coming at us in waves*. I felt myself riding these moments, just as she had.

Time would now stream on from here, as untraceably as the spit-laced tide beneath us. Paternity issues didn't figure. I laid my hand on Opal's stomach to give my reassurance direct.

I'd be there for her twins. Whatever I had was theirs.

xxviii

Opal was far from the only person I saw.

There were all my fellow workers too, and the old folk I whiled away so many afternoons with. We'd certainly laugh a lot (the class-clowning that so irked Lani came back into its own), but though I grew fond of many of them, with none did I become close.

I knew these people who lived more straitened lives saw me as a virtually alien being. That made true friendship difficult. However ready most of them were to accept or even honour me, I'd then return to the opulent lighthouse – and they wouldn't.

But I hardly found myself more at home in Opal's circle.

I've said before that she herself didn't seem to fit into any kind of company, and that remained true. Her painting, her books and music, then particularly the twins seemed to give her all the diversion she needed. But it fell within her remit as estate owner to host semi-formal dinners two or three times a year.

At these functions, when up to sixteen others would join us around her dining table, a startling amount would be eaten and drunk (smoked and snorted too, though not as a rule by Opal herself, even before she fell pregnant). Late on, we often danced, though again I myself never danced with Opal; music didn't work on us that way.

Her guests tended to be married couples: people well-placed in the world of the arts or education, a sprinkling of authority officials. They were all bright people, armed to the teeth with information, and often riotously entertaining.

Some of the regular returners ended up greeting me like an old comrade, and most came to see me as part of the lighthouse furniture. But in reality, like my co-workers, they held back, never saying around me things they doubtless felt freer saying among themselves; not necessarily disparaging things, just not for my ears, since something – for them – still set me apart.

They all, however, seemed to take a keen interest in how I kept in shape through my "regimes" of manual work and running. They'd joke that they set their clocks by the sound of me pounding past on O's empty night-time roads.

You could almost say they took a pride in how fit I kept myself. To that extent it wasn't just Opal's furniture I felt I was seen to be a part of. In me and in my continuing welfare, her whole cadre seemed to have a kind of investment.

And I must have been aware that all of them – all of us – were living inside a bubble. It was a rare dinner when someone didn't wave at the glass wall and say, 'There's another world out there'.

This was borne out when one year, at a radius of a twenty-minute drive from the lighthouse, checkpointed palisades were installed, with very little notice, to enclose our part of O.

It was from high-rises now set beyond this "pale" that most of my fellow-workers, like Opal's life-class students, were bussed in daily; and to them that I bussed myself out to perform what Opal's dinner guests referred to as "our dear Bede's good works".

Around the table there'd be lively competition to give the most extreme examples of the crimes against good taste – as well as potential new dangers – that were massing in the shanty towns beyond the emplacements.

Many of these anecdotes sailed so far over my head, I couldn't make myself sound as astounded as everyone else in response, and if this was misconstrued as disapproval, some of those nearest me might go so far as to apologize, or make wry asides about "Bede's higher standards" or "nobler creed".

'It hasn't all been plain sailing here,' they'd say self-defensively, 'but it hasn't been a total write-off!'

I'd laugh along with them, unsure if I was being told or asked. And when they did later ask me more confidentially how things were going, I sensed they didn't mean day-to-day things, nor how things were falling out just for me. They seemed to be inviting more wide-ranging comments about the regrowth, as if

I might have an insider's view, or even (as Opal too had seemed to suggest on our tours) feel a kind of responsibility.

Now and then during the dancing this might be made still more explicit: guests a good deal the worse for wear clapping me on the back and saying, 'It's you we have to thank for all this!', 'Bede our lodestar!', 'You're as good as our patron saint!'

Then they'd laugh fit to burst in such a way that I couldn't help joining in. What was in such names, after all? To her face some of them called Opal "lady bountiful" and "madame silver spoon", which she seemed to take in her stride. I don't believe anyone ever referred to her within her hearing as "the owner", though.

xxix

There was just one guest, always unaccompanied, who never took that particular line with me.

Kuno, he was called. The same name – initially to my own private amusement – as Tchure's invented cohort member, though on every count this rather older man was cut from a very different cloth from that imaginary being. He didn't go naked, he ate very heartily, and he denied at every turn that he was any kind of an intellectual.

He was also by far the highest-ranking official I met on O.

Around Kuno Opal was never more than coolly polite. But since she was not the type to have anyone at her table for the reflected glory, I assumed he wasn't there just for social reasons.

I didn't like to dwell on this, but while convalescing I'd wondered whether in the first instance I had been billeted on Opal, just as successive island communities had once been asked to take in our whole cohort. If this had been so, then perhaps Kuno exercised some form of continuing supervisory function.

I'd actually noticed him, twice, before we ever sat down to eat together, each time up on the rise where our former block stood. This was long before the night encampments were moved on, or the doors to Voormann Park Museum thrown open.

I didn't know then who he was, seated in a powder-blue convertible away from the campers but appearing to watch them closely, like someone in a security vehicle.

He watched me too as I ran past these latest little crowds, doubtless noting my pace falter as I cast my eyes over them all. Both times he gave me the kind of nod from behind his windscreen that you mightn't give someone you saw as a total stranger.

For years after, he and I seldom spoke at the lighthouse, but I was always glad to see his name on a place-setting card.

Grey-haired and sallow-skinned, dressed down but always immaculate, he was the one guest who seemed more interested in listening than in making a case, and when he did speak his voice was low yet somehow strident, like soft shouting. Had he been a few years older, I might've looked to him as a father figure.

At every dinner there would come a point, usually while someone else was holding forth over the hubbub, when I'd notice Kuno remove his gold-rimmed glasses to look at me sidelong.

There'd be real curiosity in this look, even a kind of concern. Then something more discordant would come into his expression, as if he not only sensed that we both wanted to steer the talk into different territory, but that in due course we should.

For all Kuno's easy-going urbanity at Opal's table, however, beyond it he surely inhabited a harsher world.

At one evening's end an older woman who smelled of freshly-cut freesias shook my hand in the doorway then leaned in. 'A society can be measured by the way it treats people like you!' she said, and when she saw me frown, she flushed.

'You know what I mean,' she went on. 'People who are – how to put this? – who are in the system but not really of it!'

She'd spoken in a hushed voice, but not quietly enough to escape the ears of Kuno, who was about to leave too.

'No one is *like* Reger Bede,' he said, interposing himself between us to squeeze my shoulder. 'He is unique!'

I'm not sure what played more on my mind afterwards: the woman's remark, or the fact that when Kuno put out an arm to me, I saw something dark against the white shirtfront beneath his unbuttoned jacket. At first I took it to be braces, but I then realized it had actually been a pistol in a holster.

XXX

Kuno's official title was "liaison warden", which I took to mean liaising primarily between the central authority and prefectures like our own. He seemed perpetually to be in transit, and I understood that his famously chic flat on O (where he lived during occasional secondments working from an office inside Voormann Park) was one of many such *pieds-à-terre* he owned.

In dry deference to his exalted pay grade, or even to faintly mock it, certain other dinner guests always addressed him as Warden Kuno. He seemed unfazed at being teased, dismissing his role as "covering a multitude of sins" the only time I ever heard any guest broach his specific responsibilities.

This ever-roving figure was often in my thoughts. Might he also, I wondered, be keeping tabs on communities where other ex-cohort members had settled. To say I had now stopped missing them would not be false. But I wasn't yet home free; old muscular pain can sometimes just have gone deeper. (And my people could still feel so close that it was as if they hadn't gone at all, just abandoned physical form to reach a place where a heart of light still pulsed, perhaps now as a backbeat for heavenly song.)

At least I had come to accept that the whole group couldn't have stayed intact after moving on from O, though throughout my convalescence I'd imagined every one of them still standing shoulder to shoulder both on and off the boats, with Tchure continuing to keep the book of ours while he lived out his life like a race to the finish.

Maybe this was because it was only to the entire tribe that I could imagine putting the question which never quite went away for me: why had they left without saying a word? Even if that word was just "Goodbye", and even if it came from just one of them.

Still I stood in need of that taking of leave.

As Opal approached her due date, I dreamed of making an approach to Kuno: to sound him out, enquire if he might arrange for me to touch base again with one or more of my former peers. There were even times when I told myself he might be waiting on me to do just that.

But I didn't. I couldn't. Partly because it would've felt like going behind Opal's back; partly too because the person I missed most was now beyond anyone's reach. But mostly it was because – like the cohort's procession when I was a part of that – this one-man march of my own on the reverse side of the now-flipped disc could only ever head away from the past.

Opal meanwhile dreamed dreams of her own. Dreams she never shared with me. But at one dinner more mellow than most (it must've been before the twins were on the way, since she'd just had a smoke with all the rest of us) she may have dropped her guard.

A guest had described a new stage show about first love which he had had a hand in financing. Some of the others took this as a cue to discuss what the state of being in love felt like for them, and a woman I liked challenged her husband to specify the precise moment he realized he loved her.

To derisive but good-natured cat-calling, he gave a funny answer. Then Opal put up an idea.

'Isn't it more of a process than a moment?' she asked hesitantly. 'At one point you haven't yet begun to love, then you find you've made a transition.' She let out an uncharacteristic giggle and glanced down as if to disown it. 'Like having flown into another country's air space?'

The impresario shook his head, pretending to be impatient.

'But how could you possibly know that?' he cried. 'One country's air space is just like any other's! When you're up that high, you haven't got a clue where you are unless someone else tells you!'

'Or perhaps,' came a new voice, which to even my surprise turned out to be mine, 'it's not so much a space as a place? – '

I didn't get a chance to elaborate (maybe about some altogether different dimension, the kind of place to which music might transport us), the table at once taking over.

'You mean, being "in love" is like being "in a hotel"?' the impresario's wife asked me.

'Or "in the shower"!' laughed the man beside her.

'Next time you're in love, do send me a postcard! – '

So it went on, and Opal's love-as-airspace idea was left high and dry, although not right away by Opal herself. She was sitting directly opposite me, so probably only I noticed as she sat straighter, rearranged her napkin, then murmured with a small forlorn smile which she seemed to be aiming just past my shoulder:

'Oh, I knew all right. I knew exactly where I was.'

xxxi

For two years or so after the birth Opal hosted no dinners, even though she soon went back to work, leaving the young assistant who'd been with her during the later stages of her pregnancy to become the twins' first live-in nurse. The first of many.

When the dinners resumed, Kuno no longer figured. I asked Opal why this was and she simply said he'd taken himself off the circuit. It wasn't until the night of the twins' fourth birthday that I saw him again. Or rather, in the small hours of the next day.

After my run I had slept in fits and starts, so towards dawn I pulled on my now much cleaner cohort coat, with my last locker notebook and pebble still in its right-hand pocket, and padded down to where our boats had once bobbed.

A scatter of unfamiliar vigilants sat in pairs around the terrace, all eyes on the water. I'd been standing at the curved perimeter wall for some time before I heard a car door slam, then in a gust of cologne and nicotine Kuno was beside me.

'I had people staying,' he said, scuffing out his cigarette with his heel and nodding at one of the pairs below. 'They asked to come so I brought them. Sorry if you'd expected the place to yourself.'

In the darkness I shook my head, turning Lani's pebble over and over in my coat pocket. I was pleased he was still around and looking well, if a little more drawn. Relieved, even.

'There's meant to be a new moon,' he went on. 'But I think it more likely we'll get a storm.'

Their legendary storms! I'd still known only the balmiest weather on O. Glancing at me sidelong, he reached into his well-cut jacket's inner pocket and brought out a small sheaf of folded papers as if to share something with me. Then he appeared to have second thoughts, and we went on standing in silence.

'They're following their hearts,' he said finally, nodding again at those below. 'There can't be words for everything, can there?' He turned to gaze up at the higher ground. 'But that's not for me to tell you,' he went on, directing his hushed voice away from everyone, including me. 'You being the writer.'

My blood began to pound. He may not have been referring to my time as a writer in the cohort. He'd been on O a long time; he was beadier than me. He may have seen me after my convalescence sometimes scratching a handful of my lost people's names down there in the sand, the way that Tchure had once scratched mine; or more recently, in the same spot, getting the twins to practise their alphabet.

On, my blood pounded, on.

Then as he turned back my way, for a moment he unfolded his sheaf of papers, and glancing down I saw what looked just like an offprint. One of mine or Tchure's.

It really was no more than a moment. His people were already coming up the terrace: a pair of stocky men in smart suits, lanyards around their necks. And the light was very poor.

But in terms of running heads, typeface and column-width, the page he flashed at me was indistinguishable from one of ours. Though what really grabbed my attention was that it had been comprehensively doodled over, almost all of its text blocked out with black ink. What remained at the centre was a thin trail of white space containing just a few individual words – a trail that could have been described as the outline of a heart.

Kuno would've known there was no time for me to step closer and read what the unblocked-out words, strung together in this new sequence, might have said. Plainly he didn't mean for me to try. But equally plainly he'd wanted me to know he had it, and that something may have been derived from it.

On refolding the sheaf and returning it to his pocket, Kuno locked his eyes on mine, his hand poised over his jacket at precisely the spot beneath which he'd once allowed me to see his pistol.

'When you feel ready to talk,' he told me before his people got to us, 'a time-out at a retreat can always be arranged.'

He gave me his old discordant smile.

'I just need the word, Bede. But it has to come from you.'

All three men bade me a friendly good night and I stayed where I was, a little unsure on my feet, to watch Kuno's latest model of the same powder-blue convertible purr back out to the highway.

It had to come from me, he'd said (Lani's own words to the letter), even though he would have known I was now less of a free agent than I had ever been, and he was surely just as aware that my one-man march still had a distance to cover.

As things turned out, there would be an even longer hiatus before I set eyes again on Kuno. But he'd set the marker down.

xxxii

"Don't expect miracles" we used to say in the cohort. Then the regrowth gave the lie to that. And as the twins became mobile and able to communicate, each moment I spent around them felt like the biggest miracle of all. At times I could barely breathe for entrancement. The very words "new life" never lost their sheen.

Instead of just a rain of shavings as a reference for childhood, I now had all these riches. (Though when the twins were old enough to press me for what I could remember, that episode so fascinated them that they'd make me re-stage it by drowning them in fallen leaves. "More shavings!" they'd squeal in delirium, "More shavings!")

My love for Muir and Iona subtracted nothing from my love for Opal, but it took me past her. It took us past each other. And in my case, it took me back.

The joy I felt when buried up to my neck in sand by them, or playing increasingly competitive ball games, or gluing together cardboard boxes to make robots and puppet theatres – all of this rekindled a glow I had forgotten since coming off the boats.

Memories now flooded back. Memories in the main of Lani, so absorbed by the barracks children, but who would never herself know motherhood. Had she wept that day having sensed what lay ahead for her? *It's all out there, already.*

Was it this that finally made her unable to go on living? At each day's first birdsong I'd shiver for pity at everything Lani had missed.

But I too now had some idea of what must come, a sense that my time with the twins would be limited. So all our shared moments had to count: to build us up for when we'd part.

I never of course played a major role for them. In the world as it was then, the greater share of their upbringing was always going to fall to Opal, her live-in nurses, and eventually a small army of visiting female tutors.

And since the nurses couldn't easily be accommodated at the lighthouse, the plan had long been for Opal and the twins to decamp to one of her own rental properties nearby. ("You'll so appreciate us all being out of your hair, trust me!")

Once a suitable apartment fell vacant, Opal used the lighthouse only for painting and entertaining, and this was bound to affect our dynamic. But most days when she wasn't travelling I still saw her, and she continued to spend several nights a month with me in the bolthole.

In some ways we'd been living in parallel before, but this split-site arrangement underlined it. 'All I want is for you to be happy,' she reminded me outside the lighthouse on the day they all moved out, and I never had reason to doubt that.

From the start Opal took the twins on regular long holidays outside of O, often combining these breaks with her teaching trips. With me, the three of them took more local excursions to larger resort bays, art galleries or water-sport hubs.

That's when Opal accumulated many of the family photos I alluded to earlier. Almost coquettishly she'd approach total strangers and ask if they would snap us with her camera or phone. Often she'd have a hand on my shoulder, our arms might be loosely linked: the group as we looked to others on that day.

Several times she drove us to the man-shaped cliff she had based my portrait on, and photographed me against it with the twins.

Thanks to the many popular prints and posters (all proceeds made over to charity), Opal's "iconic" painting had become synonymous with the region, though to my untutored eye the actual rock formation didn't look very much like me.

With each successive viewing, I saw instead a much closer resemblance to that "face" on the sentry-shaped cliff which had greeted us on our arrival at the island of the heart of light.

As a quartet we had many good times together. Now and then too, when the twins' tutoring schedules permitted, I'd make up a different four with the current nurse. I'd see my main job then as giving the children a little light relief, much as I had for so long in the cohort.

As smaller kids they both seemed to get my humour. I daresay quite soon the three of us were horsing around at much the same level of sophistication, and I may well have been the nearest thing they ever had to a peer on O – I certainly never saw them in other children's company there. This did change later. As a resource for them I clearly had my limits, and by early adolescence they may have seen these as long since reached.

But before then, it was on the few occasions when I might have been regarded as their main carer – by which stage they barely needed caring for at all – that we had our key afternoons.

xxxiii

The twins were developing by this point into quite a formidable and sometimes moody pair, with a keen eye for what went on around them.

'Do a lot of the people here know you, Bede?' Iona once quizzed me as we strolled through crowds of mainly bussed-in day trippers from the projects at the finally-opened Voormann Park Museum. I laughed but her less bullish brother didn't.

'Everyone knows Reger Bede,' Muir replied. 'Or not so much who he is, but who he has to be.'

They'd often talk this way as they grew older, across me, as if I didn't have to be there for them to construct their own third person. They also had their own secret language, a thing of tics and giggles as much as words, that no one else could decipher.

As for the matter of "recognition", I should perhaps say that for all of Opal's dinner-guests' talk of lodestars and patron saints, most people on O understandably showed little or no interest in me. But as well as those few who might nod in passing, presumably on account of the poster, there was always a smaller number, some on Opal's own payroll, whose expressions would tend towards the more aggrieved side of indifference we'd all become acquainted with in the cohort.

For a long period we'd trek out to Voormann Park at least once a month. As an "educator in art" Opal qualified for a transferable seasonal family pass to both house and grounds. Usually we'd visit on a Saturday, when the place was at its busiest, so that my own working or volunteering week wouldn't be eaten into, and the nurse could also take some weekend respite.

Having dropped the twins and me off, she'd drive on through the palisades to visit family or friends, leaving us to spend the next few hours on our own, with all our fellow-visitors acting in these instances as unwitting chaperones.

The great house had turned out to be a marvel of conservation, and a significant draw for museum-goers. Grand as its original incarnation had been, its later elaborations captured a series of moments in time which allowed it eventually to be billed as "a three-dimensional history of Hythe prefecture". A history in which, as I've said, our cohort's stay did not figure.

Nothing I saw in the house's interior was familiar from before, though I'd known it for only that single night. Even the caribou heads weren't in the positions I remembered. Our ground-level dressing rooms and showers had now been reconfigured beyond all recognition as a "domestic area" ranged around a central roofless "dairy court".

The faded tapestries' feasting scenes in the long gallery and the chairs made from elephant feet had some appeal for Iona. Muir was initially diverted by the house's trademark unicorns which appeared on a number of plaster friezes.

But they both had little liking for the room guides, got up in historic costume to declaim at the paying customers in cod-period language, and if they had a preference it was to stave off their boredom in the grounds, peering into fishponds or racing around the great ornate bandstand with its weather-vaned roof.

Fewer vigilants now gathered by the fences, though we'd find occasional plastic-wrapped bouquets out there.

The twins let their gaze linger on the bouquets but never asked me who they were for. I myself often came close to asking someone on the Voormann Park staff, but always finally preferred to go on imagining they'd been left in remembrance of my people. As for the twins, they'd apparently gauged – with regard to more than just the flowers – that certain questions weren't worth putting to me.

Often we'd buy food from the concession stands and take it out under the distant elms. Perhaps at Opal's suggestion they brought along art books written for younger readers, but sitting with my back against a tree-trunk, and each of them hovering close by, we'd do little more than turn the pages.

And that's where, over a period of many years, I would intermittently tell them what they and they alone seemed curious to hear. My own "new made-up stories" as they called them. Suitably expurgated anecdotes from my time in the cohort.

xxxiv

I didn't set out to regale them with my own history.

At first I tried to add to their more general stock of knowledge. For a while I could satisfy their inquisitiveness about my past by describing the jobs I'd done on O. They had a particular interest in the lobster-boats and lifeboats; I'd also faithfully pass on whatever titbits of knowledge I had picked up on our cohort's island tours of inspection.

This was how the cohort crept into our conversations. They'd pounce then on any new aspect that came up in answer to their questions: the coats, the book of ours, the girls' hooped earrings, my mimicry of some of the more distinctive voices, the catchphrases.

I did sometimes wonder if it was right to say quite so much about an era which pre-dated Opal. But there was never any sense of me suggesting it was "better". This just happened to be the time I had come alive to the world, with all its wonders and possibilities, so it seemed natural to want to pass it on.

I think what appealed to them most was our experience as a group, how we looked out for one another – our networked whole seeming to possess properties not so evident in its component parts. "The superorganism!" was a phrase Iona picked up from somewhere, around the time when I began to suspect they might just be winding me up a little.

Even so, they didn't only digest what I told them, they worked with it. I remember once sitting at a Voormann Park café table listening to them dispute whether on our travels we'd been explorers or discoverers. 'They didn't discover those islands,' Iona insisted, 'because the islands were always there.' 'Ah,' Muir replied, 'the islands were there but hidden from view, so what was hidden – or "covered" – they *dis*-covered!'

Iona looked at me, deadpan. 'I used to know that,' she said.

And much later, long after they'd stopped bringing books and started to claim that most facets of adult life just filled them with embarrassment, she would ask me in deadly seriousness, 'All those things you used to tell us – they didn't really happen, did they?'

'What do you think?' I asked her back.

Briefly her asymmetric grin reappeared from earlier in her childhood, lit up by those lovely almond-shaped eyes that were the sole feature on which the twins could be called identical.

'Maybe,' she murmured.

'I don't think even you knew,' Muir grunted, plucking up handfuls of grass a short way off. 'Sometimes you'd say "we", other times it was "they".'

Iona frowned at him.

'Well, I think it was like proper stories,' she decided, 'but then Bede put himself in them. Himself and all the others.'

Another time still, an even older Muir looked up as if stung from the screen of the latest gadget he was tapping away at, then asked me if we'd been "selected" for the boats. When I admitted that I honestly didn't know, Iona gave a snort.

'You must know,' she said. 'You made it up!'

'But did your parents actually send you?' Muir persisted.

They both looked at me so hard that they seemed as young and impressionable as I had ever seen them.

'Parents know when to let their children go,' was the only reply I felt able to give them in all conscience.

To my surprise then they chuckled, as if in relief.

'The thing with you, Bede,' said Muir, 'is that you don't quite belong on dry land. Well, not to this place anyway. You sort of only make sense in transit.'

'All this is just like a port of call for you,' Iona agreed.

'All this?' I asked.

'It's okay,' said Muir. 'We don't mind. We'd do the same ourselves.'

'We hope one day we will!'

'It's funny, though,' Muir added before returning to his screen, 'We've never really been able to see you on the water.'

After that, for years, they said little or nothing on the subject. Or on many others. For young people finding their own place in the world, this seemed natural. I felt sure any curiosity they may once have had about Opal's past life would have fallen away too, though to me Opal's life before I knew her had ceased to seem entirely real.

And so, in its way – despite the sighting I'd had of Kuno's offprint – had my own before her. More like a story I'd put myself in. Myself and all the others. Had I really been out on the water all that time? Could we ever have travelled so far in virtually self-piloting pinnaces?

Perhaps inevitably it would be Muir, one day at the Park, who'd come closest to providing an answer.

XXXV

The weather on that afternoon was particularly sultry, which didn't help improve the twins' already crabby attitude. After less than an hour they wanted to go inside for some shade.

Years had passed since last we set foot in the main residence or any of the outbuildings. But the densely-furnished interiors felt just as oppressive as before, and there were so many other visitors that there was often gridlock on the velvet-roped landings.

For some while I'd been thinking Voormann Park had ceased to be the best place for what Opal had once called our "bonding days". I wasn't sure if it was the Museum or me the twins had outgrown, but by now they really needed no more traditional minding. I could see why it made them kick their heels.

More peculiarly on that day, I was kicking my own heels too. Not to be away from the twins. Never that. Perhaps for the first time on O, I'd begun to feel a little restless in myself, though I would hardly yet have put this down to wanderlust. Maybe it was only now that I had fully come back into myself after my depletion.

We finally found a free bench on the sheltered side of the dairy court, near to the doorway to a fire-blackened kitchen. On my first and last morning there with the cohort, Jenufa would have been sitting around this same spot with her dance magazine.

When Iona needed the bathroom in a nearby annexe Muir loped along too, just as willowy as her but by now a good head taller.

I'd assumed they would need to queue, and so would take a while, but after ten minutes I went to check anyway and found a sign re-directing all visitors to a row of portable cubicles outside the oldest wing.

There, I found Iona standing alone. She said she'd told Muir to wait for her but he had vanished.

This was out of character. For all his occasional surliness the boy was a byword for reliability. Then his face appeared around an opened door set into the old wing, where vines now crept across its flaky amber-coloured stone.

He beckoned to the two of us with an uncertain smile that made him look very much like his mother.

'There's something you might like to see,' he said.

We followed him along a narrow corridor with a flagstone floor so uneven that twice Iona stumbled. Then Muir took a sharp turn through a smaller doorway to the right, where three deep steps led us all down into a tiny private chapel.

Its floorspace wasn't much bigger than my bolthole's but its ceiling must have been three times the height.

There was just an altar and some carved wooden seating, and any light that might have brightened things up through the high west-facing window was blocked out by tall, curtained scaffolding on to which a conservation firm's signboard had been fixed.

As Iona began to poke about behind me, I told them I doubted this area was open to the public. Already I found myself taking short, shallow breaths. Parts of the place were draped in snow-falls of dust, while an acrid solution the conservationists had been using raked at the back of my throat.

But it wasn't just these affecting me. A sense of anticipation was rising too. Eager anticipation, of something I knew I was going to like.

'Look,' said Muir, indicating a point on the wall near the top of the scaffolding. 'Up there.'

So I did as he asked.

I knew just what was looking back.

I've mentioned how on my last-ever island tour of inspection, "corbels" had been explained to our party: wall-projections to support roof timbers, often decorated with fantastical heads. Our guide had said that if a roof was later raised, these corbel heads could be left stranded or "orphaned". And all this, at some point, I had passed on in its entirety to the twins.

The roof in here must've been raised more than once.

The wall held three distinct lines of projections, all carved with human heads alternating with shield shapes, though not all had yet been cleaned, and some had decayed past recovery.

'The one in the middle,' Muir said. 'There in the bottom row. That's you, right? You with the others?'

He was speaking of things we'd not mentioned for years.

In the first few instants I felt very young. Had I maybe been brought to see this as a child? Then I recalled that skinny barracks schoolboy climbing his stairs of air, and I felt I was doing the same.

Because I didn't speak at once, Muir edged over to my side. Iona came up on the other. I'd started very quietly to laugh: there was nothing else for it. The whole of my life was out there waiting, and every now and then it reached back to haul me bodily forward.

This was one of those times.

xxxvi

The cliff that gave rise to Opal's watercolour was one thing, but for all the corbel's centuries of accumulated grime it really could have been me half-smiling up there. Bearded and long-haired, the only way the twins had ever known me, the way that in essence I was.

This wasn't all. The harder I looked, I could've put names to most of the other faces, bearded or not: Auber, Nguyen, Ananke, Quaye, Widsith. My eyes may have been deceiving me, allowing me to see what perhaps I now wanted to see (how many facial archetypes can there actually be?) but the head with features just like Frick's was the only one that had no hair, while the cheeks of what had to be Tchure had pinpoint indentations.

And of something else there could be no doubt.

What I'd taken for shields bore no coats of arms. Their lines were more fluid too, giving them the shapes, rather, of hearts.

There was nothing I could say to the twins, nothing that made sense. I felt both humbled and elated, buoyed by a fresh new sense of belonging, of stepping up into my own shoes.

The longer I stared at the hearts and the faces, the more of an eye-blink my time on O began to seem. Who knew how far back it all went? Had I been doing this always?

The twins were past the tactile stage but I put out an arm around each of them and neither tried to push me away.

Still I laughed in bewildered wonder, my head tilted back as if to get the whole panorama imprinted, and a welcome strength surged through me. A power of connection that came from knowing the larger procession I was a part of; this pageant was infinitely greater than any of its participants.

'So this is us!' I breathed in gratitude when at last I came back to myself, as the dumbfounded twins remembered to shake themselves free then made for the steps, the doorway.

But I'd meant them too. And I think they knew it.

The corridor I strode along after them seemed to have narrowed further. Its sunlit end looked too small for me to pass through. In this moment of strange coalescence, of still opaque illumination, I felt as large as the whole of Voormann Park.

When I stepped outside, a silent crowd stood waiting.

A staffer dressed as a cook at once closed the antique door behind me. Then she repositioned across it the length of incident tape that someone before Muir must have unfastened; it could never have been him – this just wasn't his kind of transgression.

I smiled at all my fellow-visitors looking on. I hadn't stopped smiling since the chapel. Their mood was hard to read.

Muir and Iona had wormed their way through and out of sight. But these people seemed transfixed, as if they were the ones who had just been shown the wonders inside. They could have been on the point of either panic or raising up a hymn of praise.

'I'll take it from here,' I heard someone say as he edged forward through the press, a man in a navy collarless jacket.

Kuno.

He'd lost a lot of ground since last we spoke at the inlet, and even perhaps a little of his commanding air.

He stepped right up to me, hugging what looked like an old-fashioned clipboard to his chest where a small white 'W' had been embroidered into his jacket's top pocket. His glasses hung from a short chain round his neck.

Without speaking he smiled, but when he looked into my eyes the smile faltered. Everyone behind him stayed right where they were: trippers from the projects, gaunt-faced, some still dressed in service-worker clothes, and it seemed stranger than ever to me that so many of them flocked back to O in their off-duty hours after being bussed in here daily to work.

Kuno now stood at their head like their tribune, their representative, but patently he was waiting on me.

It was as if every moment since our last exchange at the inlet had been siphoned off elsewhere. In effect he had only just set down his marker about me talking. And now I had my reply. Still with a face that wasn't quite straight, I gave him my firmest nod.

He flinched, and then inclined his head.

'A time-out?' he asked after clearing his throat.

I raised a hand in acquiescence: whatever he wanted to call it. His hollowed-out look didn't soften.

'It'll take a little while to get all my various colleagues together,' he went on. 'And plainly the hearing can't be here.'

If he was offering me one of several options, without knowing what the others were I was not best-placed to choose, but after living inside this mystery for so long, I welcomed as wide a discussion as possible. Again I raised a hand.

Kuno didn't quite click his heels together but there was something of that in the way he drew himself up.

'Leave it with me,' he said. 'You'll be contacted.'

His eyes glinted. 'And thank you, Bede. Thank you.'

He stood aside to let me pass. As he did so the onlookers moved apart, opening up a channel for me to march through on my way to where the twins sat waiting back in the dairy court.

Opal's assistant, no longer technically a nurse, was late arriving to drive us home that afternoon. A pixie-haired self-educated young woman called Anaïs, she didn't seem much older than the twins, and lately she'd been just as temperamental while serving out her notice before Opal's imminent "business restructuring".

Anaïs had always picked her way around me with borderline scorn but now, perhaps sensing something in the air, she wore the same expression I'd seen on all those faces behind Kuno. The only time she stirred herself on our homeward trip was to glance in her rear-view mirror and ask the twins if they'd done anything especially interesting at "the Museum".

I half-turned in my passenger seat to see them shake their heads. They then looked hard at each other, and in the short period left to the three of us, they said nothing to me either about what had happened that day. Nothing direct.

xxxvii

From the moment I saw those heads in the chapel, through all the time I waited for Kuno's contact, I was barely able to contain myself. It was as if everything had fallen into place, yet where that place may have been remained as elusive as ever.

Each morning I'd have the same dream. It began with me as the boy beneath the bench, shavings raining down, the high distant voice calling as if from over water. *Rayga, Rayga* – But before becoming engulfed I'd see I was in a theatre, on stage, and as the lights dimmed faces stared back at me from every seat, each one carved in stone.

After one longer-than-usual night run I went through my warm-down exercises by the old cannon emplacements. For the first time in years I sank down on my former writing rock.

Over on the curved terrace I saw by the thin light of sunrise three cellophane-wrapped bouquets wilting like tributes at an accident site. And when I then scanned the horizon, again I sensed not just "an" other world out there beyond the ramparts of this one but uncountable numbers of them, each holding a life that we hadn't quite lived, with all of these now playing out to cohere with our own in the full heart-shaped mystery of existence.

The formally-sealed letter from the authority, signed by Kuno, duly arrived. All it said was that an open-ended stay had been booked for me at a site-unspecified "retreat" (though I had always pictured with a thrill the place we had visited in the boats, with the cabins that let us live so briefly as couples).

The letter also detailed to the minute when, on a day two weeks hence, an accredited driver from the local airport would come for me outside the taverna. The fact that this date fell immediately after Opal and the twins would be leaving O for their next extended break did not strike me as coincidental.

Kuno had not said or written that any of this was to be kept from the woman who'd taken me in. But even before I knew I was to travel again, I had sensed that the more suitable time for a conversation with her might be on our respective returns.

As it was, in the run-up to her departure she already had plenty else on her mind. She seldom filled me in on her business ventures, but I'd gathered that she, like many others, was having to slim down her operation. She didn't seem unduly bothered – remarking with a sigh that few economic cycles were without their periods of contraction – but this one had an effect on all our domestic arrangements.

Refurbishments to the lighthouse had begun some time before, so that at a none-too-distant date Opal and the twins (though not, to her dismay, Anaïs) would be able to move back in. Thanks largely to the insertion of a lower first-floor ceiling, the building had already gained an extra storey where the twins would be having new bedrooms, and the spacious studio area would be subdivided into a hallway, sitting room and "family dining room". When I'd asked Opal where she planned to work when they all eventually returned, she just laughed and said, 'Oh, I'm sure I'll find somewhere!'

She also said I could stay at her apartment during the disruption, but since I was rarely home when the builders were in, this was minimal, so I'd stayed where I was, and even put in some weekend shifts myself helping with the plastering.

The twins too spent more time than was usual for them in or around the lighthouse. Twice I came back from work to find them in the bolthole. Late one evening, when I went out with the recycling, there they both were, lounging against the bins. There's a chance they may have been smoking.

'When you did sea jobs,' said Muir abruptly, 'were you ever a lighterman?' I told them no and they exchanged a glance. 'So what is a lighterman?' asked Iona. And while I said that to my understanding lightermen ferried cargo from ship to shore in small towed vessels, they watched me with widening eyes.

'The guy who took over the writing after you,' Muir then said. 'Wasn't his leaflet thing called *Lighterman, Lighterman?*'

Grinning, I told him how astonished I was that he should remember this from so many years before. They nodded at each other then as if I'd just confirmed that night follows day.

On our last afternoon together before Opal and the twins left, the four of us took a long walk to a nearby sculpture park we'd often visited before. To my surprise, armed soldiers had now been detailed to patrol the exhibits.

Opal and I had previously arranged for me to have dinner at the apartment, then stay over. To make their flight they had to be up before daybreak, so my idea was to leave just before them. Although there had still been no storms on O, the weather first thing each day had turned bitterly frosty, so as a parting gesture I planned to scrape clear the windscreen of Opal's vehicle outside her block.

The twins didn't show for dinner.

There was nothing unusual in that. When Opal realized they weren't going to come she lit some scented candles and we ate alone, but on the point of turning in (we were both still clearing the table), Muir and Iona made a disconcerting entrance.

From the shadows teetered someone tall – impossibly tall – in a long dark coat belted with twine. I saw at once the coat was mine, draped over Iona who was perched on Muir's shoulders. This composite figure's face looked far too small behind the coat's raised collar, my own filthy grey mop-head from the bolthole bathroom hanging down in place of hair, some of it tied back in a band.

Opal, smiling too widely, paused in the kitchen alcove, a half-full tagine dish in both her hands. I was still wiping down the table.

Iona turned my way, her jaw and cheeks covered by a messily felt-penned "beard". And when her mouth opened, it was only to mime, hopelessly out of synch, a word that issued from further down inside the coat: 'Archipelagonia!'

Then Muir began to lose his footing. I tore across to grab Iona before she toppled off. And as I took all her weight, Muir reached through the coat's flaps and grabbed me around the hips. For a long moment we held one another fast, three hearts hammering, then each of us started to laugh. It was just so absurd, the sort of caper we'd used to get up to in the cohort.

'Someone has to do it!' said Iona between giggles.

'You'll never be landlocked, Bede!' Muir gasped loud enough for the words to carry to Opal. And this, surely, was their point.

That Opal should hear. Our life on her patch.

I must have hoisted Iona up off her brother's shoulders, must have unknotted the twine around the coat to set her free. I remember none of that. All I see is the way Opal looked across at us, the mustard-coloured dish held up as if to protect her.

She was smiling. Opal always smiled. But her eyes seemed to suggest she was more perplexed than surprised, and I saw in them too a look of exoneration, which in the fullness of time I would understand had not been just for me.

I bunched up the coat in my fist, feeling for Lani's pebble as I did so and finding it gone.

Iona had moved to the table where she started picking at leftover fruit. The pebble was in her hand. Muir followed, lifted the mop's tangles off his sister's hair and after passing it to me, he ran the backs of his fingers down her scrawled-on face before walking from the room as if balancing a book on his head.

Turning to me, Iona held up the pebble.

'Can I keep this, Bede?' she asked. 'But not, like, forever?'

I had never discussed the pebble with them. Never told them who'd given it to me. Never mentioned Lani in all our conversations.

Opal smiled from me to her daughter, from her daughter back to me. It was the way she'd used to smile when she said, *You really have no obligation to me!* And I recalled those words now with a radically different emphasis. Had she in fact been saying all along that it was only to her that I owed nothing?

Now it was my turn to smile.

Yes of course you can keep it, I told Iona. Yes, please do.

Opal and I waited until the small hours to make love. Then before she went to shower I kissed her goodbye and stole away from her block. Up at that elevation, further from the water, I could hear more clearly the now-nightly siren wails from out beyond the palisades, punctuated by the spectral cries which for a week or so had been disturbing my sleep in the bolthole.

The heaviest frost of all had struck that night. I had a set of keys to Opal's four-wheel drive and knew where she kept her ice scraper, but I didn't need to ferret it out.

I'd have expected her windscreen to be caked with frost. Instead someone had already scraped it gleamingly clean, except for one patch directly in front of the passenger seat.

To call it a patch sells it short. The three-sided figure was a minor work of art, and it was shaped just like the heart of light.

xxxviii

There could've been any number of retreats. The one to which I was driven, flown, ferried, and then driven again along a precipitous coastal road may or may not have been the one I visited with my cohort. But I knew it on arrival, in the way that those old-time carriage-passengers would have known Voormann Park.

Yet from the moment the twin-engined plane took me up into the air from O's troop-guarded airport, so much of what followed was so far beyond my expectations that in a sense I never quite came down.

In a sumptuously-fitted self-catering cabin I was left for a week to find my own feet, or "acclimatize" as it said in the laminated welcome pack on the sitting-room's low table. Just one sighting of the sun throughout my stay would indeed have been welcome.

'We seem to have lost the weather,' Kuno said with a thin smile when finally he dropped by on the evening before we got down to business. 'You did well to bring your coat.'

With a sports bag for toiletries and running gear, that coat – now minus its pebble – was virtually all I had brought.

First thing each morning I'd wake to the faint but bracing sound of children chanting. The morning after Tchure's party on O I had heard a less distinct version, but even then it had seemed to be floating through the ether from some other, earlier place:

> *Lighterman, lighterman*
> *What do you bring? –*

That was as much as I could clearly make out, but I never saw a single boy or girl at the retreat and never really expected to. Nor did I think I would now come face to face with the person whose oddly stirring calls of *Rayga, Rayga* seemed to carry to me all the way from my own lost childhood. Yet my time with Opal already felt no more recent than my travels on the boats, and then – as time became more unstitched – even seemed to pre-date them.

On twice-daily runs I got to know the layout, hilly enough to make my circuits quite demanding. Apart from service staff in sage-green uniforms, few other people were about.

As I beat the new bounds, the out-of-season atmosphere reminded me of Opal's estate when we all first arrived. A couple of dozen cabins were dotted around, though they all stood well inside the palisade fencing with its coils of barbed wire along the topmost spikes, enclosing us on all sides and reinforced by an inner steel ring as grey as the skies above it.

The cabins' numbering followed no obvious system. The small heart-shaped boards outside their front doors could just as easily have read 64, 115 or any of the numbers up to and beyond my own, which happily was 31, just like all my cohort lockers.

Now and then I'd see officials in two-piece navy-blue outfits like Kuno's, heading into or out of the central ocean-liner building.

In the plaza where it stood I also spotted some of the other residents: for the most part elderly men wearing only towelling gowns despite the persistent chill, often using motorized wheelchairs.

None of these men was actively uncivil when I greeted them. None invited any kind of conversational exchange either. The welcome pack requested that "every fellow-resident's privacy" should be respected, so I took care to keep my distance.

Until Kuno appeared, the only person I had any kind of a conversation with was a porter in the booth at the main-road entrance. 'Now you could continue your run out there,' he called to me breezily when I once jogged right up to the road barrier. 'But we'd not be able to guarantee your safety if you did.'

He winked collusively. After chatting a while, it turned out we had someone in common. An old person I'd used to shop for, the porter's late maternal aunt. 'I can't speak for anyone else,' he said, 'but she'd never hear a word said against St Bede. Not a word!'

Before arriving I had equated this time-out with putting a gramophone into pause mode: raising the needle on its tone-arm while the disc continued to spin. But even before the talking began, it felt more like a step outside of time entirely.

Looking to sea at nights beyond the palisades, I'd see what appeared to be fires on the distant horizon. But no planes flew over, no vessels plied the waters. The sports fixtures on my TV were all on repeat from old tournaments. When the talking started too, each of Kuno's colleagues came to the cabin on what could easily have been my first and only session, always making clear that what followed should mark a fresh start.

"A new page for us all," as some explicitly put it.

And despite the sometimes disquieting silence on this clearer, much colder air, my burgeoning sense back on O that hatches were being battened down intensified at the retreat.

When, on leaving the cabin, several of my official visitors looked seaward, shook their heads and said, "There's another world out there", they made it sound like a world now in waiting, a world which could not be held back; and the expressions on their faces hinted that the transition might not be smooth.

But all this still lay ahead. After Kuno tapped on my door.

He didn't stay for long, and seemed to have a lot on his mind.

He moved around the sitting room while I stood, nudging wall pictures into alignment with the back of his index finger, asking if my "day-to-day requirements" were being met.

He paused when he saw my old cohort notebook which I'd taken out of my coat pocket and set down on the bed's counterpane. 'May I?' he asked, pointing at it. With exaggerated care he picked it up, hefted it, and flicked through its empty pages before replacing it in the exact same spot.

'This has been a long time coming, Bede,' he said on finally turning to face me. Then he glanced around and made his remark about losing the weather, smiling at me in a way that almost suggested I'd had a hand in that.

He said he would be available in his central-plaza office at any time during my stay. But if all went to plan I wouldn't need to see him there until "all the key areas" had been covered by a series of individuals who'd be coming to call on me.

'As you'll have anticipated, Bede,' he said, 'this will take the form of an extended debrief. Don't worry, your feet aren't going to be held to the fire! But the floor will always be yours. Each person who'll visit you here is an expert in his or her chosen field. They'll all be keen to hear whatever you see fit to tell us.'

I knew what he was going to say then, half in apology, half as if to cover himself as he made ready to leave.

'But it has to come from you.'

So I was to be the talker, with others simply listening.

I remembered my dream of being on stage before an audience of stone heads. And I think it was only after Kuno spoke of experts that I parked one of my wilder private fancies, that the "colleagues" he'd mentioned at Voormann Park might be a euphemism for my cohort, supernaturally reconvened.

It didn't matter.

Those boats would never be burned. In spirit my people would always be with me. And it was them – my sole point of interest for anyone else – that I'd have to talk about now.

xxxix

Over the coming days I opened my door to a stream of polite if somewhat remote visitors, most of them around Kuno's age, all dressed in the same smart navy authority-wear, all with the same embroidered 'W' motif on the left breast of their jackets.

Sometimes I might be visited three times in a day, then not at all the next. Few of them took notes and there was no cross-referencing to previous sessions, so I often found myself treading the same ground, no doubt as part of a concerted strategy.

First there'd always be a few minutes of light chat. With one tall bespectacled woman I remember discussing a TV documentary about a notorious poet we'd both watched the previous evening.

'You must be creative yourself,' she said. 'Didn't you used to write?' (This was the only time any of them referred to my membership of the cohort without me bringing it up first.)

I smiled but told her I'd only written then because I had been asked to; and that was, besides, in another lifetime.

'While you were travelling?' she clarified before giving me a slow smile of her own. 'Ah, the principal navigations!'

'Whatever comes,' they'd all then say, the way Lani described her writing. 'Please feel free to speak about whatever comes.'

And what came to me invariably concerned the cohort. Prior to opening up each time I'd have little idea what I might say. It was like being back on my old writing rocks, sitting bemused before the empty page. Then off I'd go.

Making clear that I wasn't speaking for us all, I talked not just anecdotally but also speculated on how we may have fitted into the larger cycle. And though I must have often rambled like the lonely old people I'd sat with back on O, each visitor seemed happy enough to give me free rein.

But only towards the very end, when they began to ask direct questions about more recent times, did I get the impression that anything I brought up was of more than a passing interest to them. Often they looked distracted, even glazed. All these horses, they might've been saying, have long since bolted.

With only one, the freshest-faced of the men, did I enquire about the nature of his specialism. He thought hard before telling me he was more of a generalist than some, his main focus being upon "the lifetime's narrative arc".

At the end of that session, I hesitantly put it to him that rather than an arc, I'd come to feel I was following a spiral groove, like that on a vinyl record.

'Well,' he said after another long moment, 'Good stories do tend to travel from the outside in. The centre's what we aim for, after all.' He gave me a level look. 'The heart of the matter?'

During the final sessions I was repeatedly encouraged to speak about my time on O. Had it all, they asked, panned out as I might have anticipated? Not so much with regard to Opal, but in terms of more general impressions.

If they meant the regrowth, I replied, as an uninformed layman I had no wisdom to offer. Quite the opposite. The most common knowledge seldom seemed to be held in common by me.

'But even so – ' they'd gently insist.

So then, for what it was worth, I'd give my view, though even here I used my cohort experience as a yardstick.

On our earliest travels, I explained, we saw communities of all shapes and sizes, and were treated much the same by each. There hardly seemed to be haves and have-nots, since no one back then had had two beans to rub together. You could therefore believe (as most of us did) that when the regrowth brought plenty, its fruits would be shared out equitably –

I remember one visitor leaning forward when I paused here, a point I had reached previously with at least two of his colleagues.

'And you feel this was not delivered?' he asked.

Surprised by his interest, I was tempted to shrug and apologize for seeming so wet behind the ears. I almost did. He was too far away to reach out and give my arm a rallying shake, but his smile implied that perhaps he'd have liked to.

'There are levels at which we are all in the dark,' he said. 'At some of them we know much less than you. Please do go on.'

So I did, comparing Opal's lighthouse dinners with our cohort's occasional big meals, when each table in our blocks' refectories had similarly seated around eighteen.

At Opal's evenings, I said, society beyond our bubble was hardly, if ever, discussed. Society in the round. And outside of that bubble too, as far as I could see, the less privileged seemed to lack the time and leisure to be able to re-imagine, as a whole, this world they all had to labour so hard to sustain.

The man opposite began to nod.

Now obviously we in the cohort were callow, I said, but in our own debates we'd almost always focus on some more widespread good, or as Uluru would say, "a tide that'll rise to lift all boats!"

My visitor lowered his eyelids. 'The young,' he said, 'can always be relied on to set the world to rights over a communal meal.'

All these years later I felt barely more sophisticated than I'd been back then. 'But – ' I owed it to my younger self to struggle on.

But out there in the regrown world of O, I told him, so much had been built four-square upon a remembered, recorded past, its builders for the most part seeming to pick up where they had left off before the blackout, since for them all the older information still lay to hand.

Yet did that really amount to "not in the old way"? To me, this veered closer to recreating Voormann Park in such loving period detail that it ran the risk of making a fetish of the past, maybe as a way to keep at bay a more intractable present.

The other man pursed his lips. He asked in what "new way" this "atomization" I had seen all around me in Hythe prefecture might have been headed off. To which I had no answer.

'It's just that in the cohort,' I felt driven to tell him anyway, 'we'd forgotten so much that each of us constantly had to dance around all the gaps in our own life-stories. And yet this was precisely what helped us to choreograph new and perhaps unexpected routines that were common to us all.

'In that sense,' I asked him back, 'could our limited memories perhaps have been a gift: something to build on? And in the same way that a door closing really can make a room seem bigger, perhaps at times it's at least worth trying to construct from a cornerstone of thin air?'

I can't honestly say how that was received.

Though I gazed at the official, I was seeing how my cohort had gone up into the heart of light, with the promise of just such a new way waiting there and possibly not just for us. I had to wonder if some of the old scepticism which we always felt was aimed at us had to do with the fact that we didn't "deliver".

What if it doesn't turn out any better next time? the drunken manager at the barbecue had shouted. Others maybe shared that attitude, not least my fellow residents here, who now turned their backs as I ran by. One of them had even spat.

But I wasn't thinking just of our elders. A generation would've grown up imbibing "not in the old way" with their mother's milk. If they'd caught wind of our cohort too, had they seen us as synonymous with that slogan's sense of fresh purpose?

And did this explain why in the end Anaïs, for example, behaved around me as if she'd been sold a false bill of goods: having seen me as part of a "Light Bringing" group whose mere existence once implied all manner of progressive change?

'Well, I think we're just about done here,' my visitor was saying.

He meant just that session, not the whole protracted process. But whatever the value of this time-out to anyone else, I'd started to feel I had been away too long from O. And what happened next convinced me I had to get back.

xl

I'd appreciated right away that my cabin bore the same number as all my lockers in the cohort's residential blocks. While running I'd keep my mind alive by nosing out cabins I had not yet mentally ticked off, then try to remember which cohort members had been allocated the corresponding locker numbers.

Plenty were tucked away, even camouflaged, in improbably inaccessible spots. And on these runs there was one cabin I was particularly keen to see. In the end I found it: 42, the number of the locker Lani always made for on arriving at a block.

I'd probably have gone on missing it, had I not one heavily overcast morning seen a tall woman climbing a zig-zag path up to where it stood, previously obscured from my view by a large knuckly yew tree.

This resident, who soon vanished, had her back to me, but her step was supple, and she wore a short corduroy jacket of a strikingly similar green to Lani's old ankle-length coat.

I ran past the foot of that path regularly afterwards.

It was a game. No more than a game. The resident's way of moving, adjusted for age, had also been very much like Lani's, and as Lani herself used to point out, walks are as unique as fingerprints.

But the longer I didn't spot her again, the more I dwelt on the fact that I had never seen Lani lifeless. Until at last I paused at the foot of the steps, stooped to pull out a tiny clump of weeds, and then started weeding further up the flight.

This was early one evening after I had just described my continuing regret over having lost the cohort so abruptly. 'With people who were once so important,' I'd said, more to myself than to the woman opposite, 'it helps to be able to say goodbye.'

When the weathered porch of cabin 42 came into view, I could see from below that its front door was ajar. And when I came almost flush with the cabin's outer wall, I saw that the window, like the door, was not fully closed. Thin banners of escaping patchouli smoke unfurled on the cold air.

Archipelagonia! –

I climbed higher to the threshold – and in the moment I saw her sitting cross-legged beneath a clothes rail with her palms turned out, just before our eyes could meet, I wished I had thought to come in my coat. Even without the pebble in its pocket, if I had been in my coat I was sure it would've been more appropriate.

It took no more than a split second. I was backing away, hands held high in apology, almost before taking her in: this much younger woman with eyes so much paler than Lani's.

There was no outrage in her expression. I'd even have called it impassive apart from those eyes, telling me that we of course had nothing whatever to say to each other. And though she was lovely, the elements of her loveliness resolved themselves only when I was back in my cabin, curled around my notebook on the bed, with the children's chants once again circling.

Yes, there had been Lani in the young woman's colouring, her bone structure. Something too in the firm set of her mouth. But the line of her nose, the slope of her forehead – these I knew from countless reproductions of Opal's painted version of my own face. The girl in cabin 42 could have been the child of Lani and the rock man of Opal's imagination. And even on my cabin bed hours after the whole thing happened, I would still have taken a "goodbye" from her in lieu of all the others.

The next afternoon I went, without an appointment, to see Kuno.

From the plaza building's reception area they waved me straight up, and through a doorway I saw him seated behind a wide teak desk, reciting metrics into a phone, his fingers bridged up like a snooker player's to hold a small stapled document open.

He waved me in while he finished his call, indicating that I should close the door behind me. I didn't take off my coat.

The office was oddly impersonal: no photos, no wall decorations. I crossed to the window and stared down two floors at a pair of magpies who had the run of the plaza.

There was a hypnotic quality to the way Kuno went on delivering his figures, as if spinning out airy little clouds of them to float up and break apart against the harsh fluorescent tube above our heads. Before signing off he used the phrase "foreseeable future", one I could never imagine passing my own lips.

'So,' he said at length, rising and directing me to a nearby tub-shaped office armchair. 'Time to move on?'

I turned to the chair but stayed on my feet by its side, going through the motions of thanking him for all the expense and expertise directed my way, just as I'd felt Kuno and his colleagues had gone through the motions with me.

'We've always tried to do our best for you,' Kuno said, and it was hard not to hear ambivalence even there. 'We thank you in return. Your personal perspective has been invaluable.'

I smiled and said surely not! Particularly on the way things had turned out on O – wouldn't anyone have said the same as me?

Taking off his glasses and rubbing one eye, Kuno nodded.

'Perhaps,' he replied. 'But someone does have to say it. The right person, at the right time.' He refitted his glasses. 'And it does depend on how it's said.'

His look relayed the last words for him:

It has to come from you.

193

He lowered his eyes then, as if a line still to be crossed had been drawn on the carpet between us. He looked profoundly tired, worn down, reaching the end of his own road.

A magpie from the plaza clattered up onto the windowsill, and on spotting it, Kuno gave a start.

'I saw the person in cabin 42,' I told him.

'Yes,' he replied, still following the bird with his eye. 'Yes, you would've done. And she, along with our current handful of other residents, will have seen you.' He paused to stroke his nose. 'I don't doubt that some of them will have been boorish.'

I said nothing. The magpie seemed to watch him back.

'It is in the nature of these things. They've all had their own pictures of how life might unfold for them. You often hear it said: "Not everything's black and white", although in the last resort so many things are exactly that. Both black and white. Dark and light.'

We watched the magpie take off, as if primed.

'Yet people do like to see just one or the other. Especially if things don't fall out quite as they had hoped. And we have to know, don't we, when to bring the curtain down on the whole show? So the next ones through can try it their way?'

He eyed me then with a look close to trepidation.

'But please don't feel it's you they are registering their disappointment with, Bede. It's really nothing personal.'

As if recalling time was short, he moved to the door.

'I mustn't keep you,' he said upon opening it. Then he didn't let go of the handle. 'That notebook of yours,' he went on, gesturing at the coat pocket where I always kept it.

'Who knows how useful it might be henceforth if you were to put down in writing what you've told us about yourself?'

'In the cohort?' I asked, following him across the floor.

'And subsequently, as you've continued on your course. An overview of the whole cycle? Get it all down in one place – '

He made it sound like an afterthought but couldn't disguise the edge in his voice.

I wasn't initially sure. I'd never imagined going back to writing. And couldn't his colleagues just have transcribed what I'd told them? But as I looked through the doorway, the air seemed to rise and part to present a different, brighter corridor. *Rayga,* I heard. *Rayga –*

And although no one was there, I saw as if in photographic negative a figure: the woman I'd first sensed in the days after Lani died. As soon as I saw this, it was gone. Light, figure, all.

Dazzled and disoriented, I heard myself accept Kuno's suggestion, but also ask what I might do with the finished book.

'You'll know,' said Kuno, gripping my shoulder and exerting substantial pressure to move me out. 'You'll know because it's yours. Yours so it can be ours!'

'Forward, Bede,' was the last thing he called after me as I walked away, his voice now as thin as a rattle. 'Always forward!'

It sounded urgent, an instruction to be followed for as long as it took me to leave him behind. Not to turn back, however tempted I felt. And while on one level he couldn't seem to get me off his hands quick enough, on another I knew he'd devoted his life to me – him and many like him – so the way I saw it now, the least I could do was comply.

The low percussive crack I heard half way down the stairs could have been a pistol shot or just the slamming of a door.

Still partly dazed by what I had glimpsed in the corridor, a tremor passed through me but I didn't check my step before exiting the building to find a car already booked to take me on.

xli

On the return flight to O, even at low altitude, all sight of the sea was soon lost through my small aircraft's window.

Intermittently the central TV screen tracked our plane's dotted-line progress against a less parched artwork version of the rolling plains below, giving way finally to a series of vast urban settlements.

Our destination of Hythe prefecture was presented as the tip of a huge landmass.

"Temporary inclemency over the south of the prefecture" delayed our night-time touchdown by hours. Finally then: a fabled storm.

While waiting to descend, the lack of lights below suggested we were in a holding pattern above an uninhabited seaboard to the north.

I was in a holding pattern of my own.

Sometimes when a gramophone disc is put on pause, the needle comes back down slightly later in the track, and after my time-out I'd assumed I would not be going back to the same world I left. I kept reflecting on how everyone at the retreat had discussed my time on O as an era already passed. Everyone including me. It was as if I'd had to be drawn away so events elsewhere could rush on in my absence, making the whole of my stay nothing more than a luxurious diversion, a pause in a theatrical production for the changing of a stage set.

As day broke, a few features emerged below: wind farms, derelict fantasy mansions with candlesnuffer roofs, forests, parched plateaus. No sign at all of any conurbations.

The colours were like those in the child's atlas I used to watch the twins pore over with their nurses. Watery brown highlands rising out of the green like tea-stains on a plucked-up tablecloth. The ocean's turquoise fringed by paler blue shallows – the same tones as my cohort's mornings full of old light and undimmed hope. The colour of many of Opal's canvas washes.

Once we were down, there were more security personnel than travellers at the airport. 'We needed that old blow-through,' I heard a baggage-handler say to one of the gun-toting officers, 'though you never know what it'll have knocked out.'

On leaving the terminal, outside which a female driver waited beside the same car I'd begun my outward journey in, I caught a new scent on the much cooler air, a distinct bolt of wet lavender. It made me think of how on walks with Opal before she had the twins she'd drag her artist's fingers through aromatic shrubs then thrust her hand sideways under my nose. So characteristic a gesture, wanting to share yet seeming to push away.

Even as the last leg of my journey to the lighthouse began, I felt I had already overshot. Nor could I put the unfamiliarity of so much of the passing scenery down to the amount of complimentary liquor I had accepted while we circled.

Outside the taverna white plastic chairs lay strewn on their sides beneath the tables. Many of the smaller palms projected out of the soil as if they were about to be launched at a target.

The taverna's doors were still open from the night before. Chalked on a board outside was a general invitation to "Come in and help us clear all stock! Everything must go!"

To fortify myself for what might lie ahead I went inside. A patron I'd never seen before directed me to a makeshift new bar in the TV lounge where half a dozen black-tied men and a pair of women in close-fitting long dresses sat quietly smoking at a table.

From a liveried girl (who like the others gave no sign of knowing who I was) I bought a bottle of beer drawn from an ice tub now awash with lukewarm water. Only on my way out did I notice my portrait was gone. More than gone.

Unpaled by years of sunlight, an oblong of bare painted wall stood out more starkly than the picture ever had. Its absence made me feel more light-headed than all the alcohol.

'The painting that used to be up there,' I made myself ask the girl who was now decanting liqueurs. 'Is it going to be put up somewhere else?'

My question coincided with an avalanche of empty bottles into bins outside the opened back door, so I had to repeat it. The girl's bewildered smile just became more dazzling, making her lavish shrug appear highly professional. 'Is there anything else I can help you with?' she asked as I turned again to leave.

A single rowboat I knew well was moored at the foot of the inlet terrace: the poky floating kennel I'd seen from the oblique perspective of my bolthole window. But as I walked past it now, I saw how relatively – even attractively – roomy it was.

I was glad of my coat as the breeze freshened off the sea. Dawn here still appeared to be breaking. Everything looked sodden but as far as I could see no rocks had flown.

The scaffolding was all gone from the lighthouse, where a pale orange light glowed at a middle-storey window.

Through the early-morning murk the door to my bolthole was barely visible. When I tried it, I thought at first it had jammed. But it was locked, and I hadn't brought my key.

The view through the side window showed nothing I recognized. The entire living space had been turned into a repository for unused building materials and a range of expensive-looking tools.

Opal's vehicle stood on the now more deeply gravelled driveway, its bonnet still warm to the touch, so I climbed the lighthouse steps to where a bottle of fine carbonated wine with a raffle ticket taped to its neck propped the front door open.

Not wanting to wake the twins, I didn't use the bell. After no one responded to my light tap I stepped inside.

Thanks to the new partition walls I had to take a mazy route through to the glass wall. Looking out to sea there, sports bag slung over my shoulder, I drew myself up, thrusting my hands deep into my coat's pockets to pull it in tighter around me.

The light above the water continued to seem thin, tiredly simmering, like light left behind from the previous evening, not the kind of light that might ever gather.

Two people laughing quietly together sounded from just overhead. A creak then of stairs.

Briefly the light bloomed as I turned.

I used to know this.

Opal appeared with a man's black jacket draped around her shoulders, scissoring so smoothly into view that she could have been oiled, her unaccustomed make-up roaring across the floor at me in the slipstream of her perfume.

She stopped in the doorway, six steps distant.

Under the jacket were the dress and jewellery she must've been wearing the previous night – the black-and-green dress from Tchure and Ute's engagement party, the same gold bangles. We could have been revisiting that evening, perhaps to make it unfold now in the way she would always have preferred.

The waves beat on behind me as we confronted each other.

The years had caught up with Opal but now at last she was smiling freely, the old aura of loss around her quite gone. Yet the silence around us was charged with echoes of all the many breaks in our conversations. Breaks or breakdowns.

Then I heard a second set of footsteps on the stairs. Heavier, less rhythmic.

xlii

I saw him through the doorway on his way to the kitchen. White shirtsleeves, whitening hair, a loosened black tie around his neck but no shooting stick indoors.

Without looking in my direction, as he passed behind Opal he slid an appreciative hand over her hip beneath the jacket's hang. His jacket. His tuxedo. The tuxedo Opal must have offered to me on the night my people went, then kept for him in storage.

Still she smiled – at me, but because of him. The full unsuppressed smile I'd only ever known how to displace.

I heard him run a tap. Then a loud spill of cereal into a bowl.

There should have been marimba music. It could have been dusk falling now, with the streetlamps yet to come on. When I'd seen him pace through he seemed to be absorbing what little light we had – from the window, from Opal and me.

She nodded, close to laughing, eyes full of tears.

'Parr didn't know you'd gone,' she told me. 'He just came back. The way I always hoped he would.'

She had to pause to gather herself.

'But thank you,' she said. 'Thank you so very much.'

I dug one hand deeper still into my pocket, forgetting in the moment that I wasn't going to find Lani's pebble there.

'That old coat!' said Opal, knuckling away her tears and managing not to smudge her mascara, but again her eyes filled.

In the kitchen Parr was clashing glasses and crockery so loudly that even if I'd had anything to discuss with her, we wouldn't have been able to make ourselves heard. And maybe this too had always been at the heart of our compact.

O had never been anything more than a temporary roost in my own migration. I had to see that. The twins must've seen it; maybe everyone else had too. That didn't take the jolt away.

I nodded, on the point of thanking Opal back, but when suddenly the cacophony of Parr's breakfast preparations ceased, what I heard myself say instead was, 'I want you to be happy'.

Opal's mantra, and now I saw why she had fallen back on it so often: the sound of a person who'd grown too used to losing, yet shrank away from passing on her own bad luck.

It was over. This period of my life. I'd ceased to belong.

Yet stunned as I was by the sense of loss at everything I would now have to leave behind, I felt a little lighter too.

Forward! I heard Kuno say.

I went to her to take my leave.

Perhaps because Parr was so near, her embrace felt gauche and fluttery, more like a frisk, though her hands went nowhere near the only item that mattered, the last ring-bound locker notebook in my coat's right-hand pocket.

'You'll find a few more things in the boat,' she murmured as she ran her palm down the thick strap of my sports bag.

I looked past her into the kitchen and Parr met my eye: skillet in hand, neither crowing nor confrontational. With his strong features still echoing Opal's, but the age-discrepancy now less obvious, I could see how well he fitted here. For all I knew, he might never have gone away if it hadn't been for me.

I kissed Opal's neck, stopped the black jacket slipping from her shoulder, then left for a boat that would be fitted out with what amounted to food, water and a hammer-shaped tool.

With each step I took away from the lighthouse, I could only marvel harder at how this had all been dovetailed together.

At the retreat I'd talked of the past being fetishized on O. What I hadn't grasped was that Opal herself had always been in hock to history, and for her the past was more than just a museum to wander around in. In her case it came back, and just as one purpose of her portrait of me may always have been to shape a bolder patch of colour on a taverna wall (and my own depositions – written or spoken – had maybe formed just a pool of words for others to glean for meaning), so in taking my time-out I must have helped to make this happen.

On the point of descending the terrace, I saw a convertible just like Kuno's parked a short way up the road, its engine turning over, honey-coloured headlights throbbing through the gloom.

I paused to hoist my bag higher on my shoulder, but all I could see through the windscreen was the tip of a lit cigarette. It could have been anyone. The car could have been a standard-issue model for authority officials. With a token salute I continued on down.

That's when two people I hadn't seen on the tiny landing stage below stood up and came forward from the shadows.

Still wearing their night clothes, they stood before me in the dim sandy light of that arrested dawn, eyes clear, heart-shaped pale flashes painted on to their right temples, both of them holding small plastic bottles of water.

First Iona stepped up to embrace me, then her brother joined us. As with their mother it felt perfunctory, but in quite a different way. We seemed to be missing a fourth person – not Opal, though I couldn't yet have said who instead. But for the three of us here, now, this was no one's idea of goodbye.

I'm not sure which of them made a point of resting a hand on my pocket that contained the notebook, as if to check it was there, safe and ready to be put to use.

They stood back and I smiled at them, remembering Muir's dear little bean-shaped head when he'd been so much smaller, and Iona's way – when not much older – of clinging bodily to my leg as I walked along and looking up at me and saying, "I'm your plaster-cast".

I'd loved them so much then and no less now.

When long ago I had told them that parents know when to let their children go, I'd largely been speaking in hope. But in whatever relation I stood to this pair, I knew they were releasing me.

They stood together on the landing stage to watch me cast off. Neither waved. I thought at first that Iona was holding up Lani's pebble to me, but in fact her right hand was empty.

She'd raised it in an unfamiliar gesture: thumb and index finger extended at ninety degrees, her thumb pointing toward her temple flash, making it look as if she had grown a single horn. Muir was doing the same.

Rayga, Rayga sounded already across the water, from a source I could no longer be quite so sure lay in my past. But as I lit out now to complete my own cycle, it had to be arguable that I had always been heading for the place where this all began.

It's also possible that once I'd manoeuvred the kennel boat a short way out to sea, whoever was in the convertible flashed its headlights, twice, before accelerating away and out of sight.

4

xliii

Who knows where the time goes? Tchure had liked to ask. The more time I ate up, the less of it seemed to pass, but only on a minute-by-minute basis. At each day's close, what I'd call the broader past appeared to have receded much faster than the present had inched forward. Yet I sensed my own "personal" time sluicing on ahead to the end of this new world, to pool there until I arrived. And even when my route seemed to take me all around the houses, I had no doubt I was following the necessary course. We used to joke about being on a mission; in all humility, it did feel that way now.

Almost at once there was land. A fresh archipelago of islands too small to have figured on my plane's in-flight route map. Every one of them had been evacuated.

I soon got the picture.

Any home with a bouquet of dried flowers pinned to its front door was in effect an almshouse, open and available to me, with a private generator primed to supply months' worth of light, heat, freezer-food. There'd be music and films on disc, stacks of washed and ironed clothes I had no trouble fitting into.

There were also books and magazines if I wanted them but no TV sets, and every last radio was dead. Nor were there any mirrors or shaving materials. No sharp objects.

While there was now no sun to speak of, I was drawn ever deeper into the sunset regions of the west, tracing the same kind of logic to which our cohort girls must once have responded.

At times it even seemed that in line with my next landfall, the distances between islands were being adjusted as I travelled, with dry land always in sight when the thin gauzy daylight started to fade: first the many islands, then the coast of the great west-facing peninsula where ultimately I would put myself among people again.

The seas meanwhile were as empty, and appeared as millpond-calm, as they had been all those lifetimes before, though undetectable currents meant I seldom needed to row. When I did, the boat which I never stopped thinking of as Parr's handled admirably.

Among the few extra items left for me inside the boat was a small selection of pens. I had no proof, but liked to think this was thanks to the twins and not Opal. None was white with a circular shaft like the old charity biros, but each served its purpose just as well.

With only one notebook to fill, albeit a thick one, at my island stopovers I wrote thumbnail small. Small, and after so long, very slowly. I might spend a week on a single pigmy paragraph, or a day-long session deciding on nothing more than where one numbered section should end before I started the next.

I tried to recount my life's post-blackout events in the order they unfolded: a continuing "towardness", as I saw it, to match my direction of travel. And just as Opal once kept photos of the twins to hand while she worked, I'd imagine their faces while I wrote – in that way not quite letting them go, even as back on O they'd be turning into young adults I would soon have barely recognized.

I was still only scratching the surface – making a mystified record not a reckoning – but where in the past I'd often felt drained by the act of writing, it now proved quite invigorating. Likewise the circuits I ran from the bouquet houses took less out of me than my most recent runs on O and at the retreat. The writing and running fed off each other.

I had always loved the idea of a second wind. As this one gusted me closer to my destination (a place I must always have known to be there, a proper place – like one of the twins' proper stories – for me to put myself in), I felt my one-person procession pick up pace.

But I wasn't just being acted upon. There was inner change too.

Soon after the twins were born, I remember the women around Opal saying her "milk had come in". Without obvious external agency, something not present before had manifested. I don't know how this felt to Opal – I'd not have dreamed of asking – and mine was of course no comparable miracle, but my old familiar body was now not quite the same.

Something different was there, in me but not primarily for me.

xliv

Since some of the new archipelago's last islands lay just off the mainland, long before resuming contact with the world I was able to observe its people from a distance.

From out beyond the lobster-pot buoys I tracked a frayed coastline of high cliffs and deeply-incised estuaries. I saw ruined lengths of town wall, steeples and shabby caravan parks, dilapidated warehouses and very few cars.

I'd watch nights fall faster over this peninsula than over the islands, then hardly any artificial illumination picked it out. By day too its inland hills were bathed in unfamiliar registers of light: pearlescent, undercharged.

After O, this looked less like a new world waiting than a quarantined corner of the oldest backwater. As its great ochre cliffs stretched on and on, it looked neither forbidding nor hospitable. Profoundly placid rather, a whole land becalmed – and oddly, still not quite within my reach, as if seen through a viewfinder. I felt obliged not just to go ashore, but to work myself closer in stages.

For a long while at the widest river-mouths I gave the boat over to the tidal flows and let myself be swept upstream until it was time to turn. Then I'd surrender once more to the pull of the open sea.

Passing and re-passing the minuscule river ports, I sat as still as a man made of rock. No other river traffic passed beneath these arched bridges. The quays and jetties stood cleared as if in readiness, all poised on the cusp of a new state of suspension.

And I used to know this too. This sense of the furniture having been moved back, the collective intaking of breath.

I'd see many more women than men, mostly with their young. Babes in arms, in some cases toddler grandchildren dressed in pint-sized overcoats. Small school-aged groups in matching outfits were walked two abreast by female minders along the riverbank or towpath.

Half-turned towards the river, these women tended to look past me, as if to check for a frothy wake behind a boat they must've known would be too small to disturb their water. Some of the older kids fixed their eyes on me, though.

They'd move their lips before looking away, but not – I think – to make any sound. One or two would slowly raise their right hands in the gesture I'd seen Muir and Iona use – forming, as I came to see it, the capital letter 'L' with a raised thumb and index finger.

Late one afternoon I watched a crocodile of singing five- or six-year-olds tramp along a bankside, shepherded by three women.

The two bringing up the rear were in later middle-age. The third, maybe twenty years younger with cropped hair, walked backwards to conduct the songs and rhymes with great gusto.

It was her own voice that struck me first. Light and high, unselfconsciously pretty. When I looked more closely, her left leg seemed a little stiff, but when she surprised me by suddenly spinning around in mid-air, her forward stride was agile, fast and full of energy.

Seeing and hearing this woman with her Tchure-like vim really galvanized me. Alerted by her voice, the moment had seemed to rush up from somewhere else entirely: the way she'd turned was so quick, so convulsive, yet the more times I re-lived it, I saw sensuality too.

It encouraged me to stop looking quite so often over my shoulder at the occasional pale fireglows which painted the low night sky back east – these too seen as if through a viewfinder, or even projected onto a screen. Forward now. Always forward.

At the next coastal town I finally put in and soon found a seafront bouquet house. An end-of-terrace two-up two-down with propane gas for power and a wealth of music on a battery-operated cassette player.

Rocks to sit and write on spilled down directly from its tiny back yard, and I stayed there for weeks, stretching to months. From then on I made all but a handful of stops on this mainland.

In each town the locals left me to my own devices, even when for a little cash-in-hand and extra exercise I took on paid work.

For my fellow-workers, mainly older men, I was so much of a sideshow to their own lives that I might just as well have still been out there in my kennel-boat, hopping between the islands.

I'm convinced they didn't set out to exclude me or conceal anything, but assumed I could never be on their wavelength. So I learned little from them; not even, for certain, the peninsula's name. Most people knew it as Calentura, but one foreman said he'd heard that "under the new circumstances pertaining" it was now officially being called, again, by its capitalized last letter alone. None of the towns I stayed in displayed their names either.

I felt I was at the edge of nearly everyone's range of vision, a sketchily amused glance seeming to elicit all they wished to know. But I was never turned away on applying to join a work team. Fishing with seine nets, stockpiling peat, manufacturing alcoholic drinks through fermentation, dismantling phone masts, spreading seaweed and shells over fields to work against the acid in the soil.

There were cavernous waterfront bars where I could get a good meal and occasionally rent a cheap, reasonably-furnished room for weeks on end. These were shabbier and narrower than any mainland bouquet house, but they brought me closer to being again in some kind of social swim, and most were easy enough to write in.

After a day spent lifting or spreading, the words often came more fluently, though seldom any thicker or faster. In the slowest times I'd close my eyes, zone out and trawl the ether for details of talks with Lani or Opal which I felt sure still hovered there indestructibly. But even if all I then picked up was an indistinct voice through the room's thin wall, or the softly beating sea, this too could be grist to my mill.

It all added up.

xlv

When I stayed in any bouquet house long enough, I'd eventually be offered company "on site". Each of the women who came, my own age or older, would let herself in only during the night while by day our paths seldom crossed. A number of them had that same air of loss, bravely borne, which at the last I'd seen disperse from around Opal.

Conversation was never at a premium. But though this latest instalment of my preferential treatment had to belong with the door bouquets and universal sage-green bed linen – a mutual entitlement it'd soon be difficult to go without – there was genuine kindness too.

When one woman thought I was sleeping, she sometimes breathed into my neck, "Not just you now, not just you" – talking either to herself or to every pair of partners who'd ever shared a bed.

A second woman, stylish and careworn, would whisper, "Good things, quietly". Pendahui, she was called. She had to repeat her name for me when I asked, looking just past me like the women I'd seen on the riverbank, as if a prompt sheet was pinned to the bedpost.

I found myself holding her closer as she slept. I'd call what we did making love, not at all in the same vein as making do or making believe. When each night began its long, slow and eventually incomplete fade into morning, Pendahui would run her hand down my arm and murmur that she had to be getting back.

'It's my kids,' she explained near the end. 'They've never had to start a day without me.'

Each of the women, I think, must've been a mother. No men in their lives at that particular time, but still and always children. Neither Pendahui nor anyone else asked my own name, nor where I was going or why. Starting from scratch and staying at scratch.

We kept on beginning right up to the end. All the ends.

Phora was initially my most reticent visitor. But she alone took some interest in my writing. 'You're welcome to look inside,' I laughed when I noticed how often she eyed the notebook on the bedside table.

Several times I did then hear her sifting through its pages at my side when she couldn't get back to sleep.

I was reminded of Tchure coming to see me on O, as if to keep track of my progress. In their different ways, was each of these women now serving some similar semi-official purpose? That may not have been all. This felt once again like a time of transaction. With each encounter, each conversation, it was not just me moving forward.

Phora slipped away earlier and earlier. When she arrived soon after one midnight, I told her she needn't feel obliged to come at all if commitments elsewhere were making things difficult. 'You're acquitted!' I told her across the tiny bedroom with a smile.

She laughed her sad soft laugh, ganging up with herself against the rest of the world. 'Don't you think it helps,' she said, coming over, 'if we aim to keep alive what light we have left?'

She cupped my now bush-bearded face between her hands, raising it until I saw tiny distant versions of myself in her eyes, then swooped down to press the whole lean edgy length of herself into me until day broke.

But an hour after leaving, she returned with tall brown paper bags full of ingredients to cook me a hero's breakfast.

In the kitchen I asked if she didn't have children waiting.

Again that soft laugh.

'Ah, they've been and gone. Flown the nest!'

I said she didn't look old enough, afraid I'd touched a nerve.

'Everyone goes,' she went on, rolling a huge tomato in her palm. 'Even down here, where we're already so far away from the epicentre.' Turning to the cooker, she blushed. 'And then they forget where they came from in the first place!'

Fiery points rose across my shoulders. Then she grinned.

'But they've got to forget, our children, haven't they? That's probably one of the main reasons we have them.' She picked up the pan and studied its emptiness. 'To do some of our forgetting for us. Unlearn some of the things we made such a mess of. Unsee us.'

After thanking her for the sumptuous plateful which I swiftly polished off, I referred back to her remarks about needing to forget. In my last notebook entry I'd written about just that, and was curious to know if she'd been throwing my own words back at me.

She touched my shoulder. That laugh. Another blush.

'Oh!' she said with a rifle-sight narrowing of one eye. 'Your writing's so small, and I'm too vain to bring my glasses! I just find it restful turning pages in the dark. It's – well, it's like counting sheep!'

When she bowed her head at the way that sounded, we both laughed so hard we ended up back in bed, but this was the last time she came to the house, so on I travelled.

xlvi

Phora had every right to use my writing as an aid to sleep, but out and about afterwards I'd look closer at how people read. Through lighted windows, on passing open-backed trucks, under breakwaters. It went beyond wondering who might eventually read whatever I produced.

On one regular run I'd use as my turning-point a former railway bridge near some close-packed housing. I would time my dusk arrivals to spot a man sitting in his garden on a green metal bench which must once have been angled to catch the last of the day's sun.

Not much younger than me, with a fizz of tightly-curled hair, he'd hold his book at arm's length, which could have made him seem sceptical, but by turns he'd look cheered, enchanted, outraged. It was as if the book itself demanded this distance, to get its reader into clear enough focus for a debate to take place, man and book seeming equal.

They'd engage until darkness fell, and even then, to get fresh light, the man kept flicking up his left foot to re-activate the heat-sensitive security lamp on his house's high back wall.

Witnessing this intermittent light stirred in me what could have been a childhood memory: a man with a similarly engaged face turning my way as we cycled together to a railway station.

We were riding through the night at speed, with an urgent sense of him "getting me out", "sending me on ahead". I had no lamp on my own child's bike, but as long as he kept moving forward, his dynamo cast enough heart-shaped light down on to the road for us both.

My eyes would begin to prickle as if in recall, but however many times I tried to merge this figure with the man whose legs I'd grabbed beneath the bench, nothing more would surface.

The only figure to gather any definition was the woman with her plaintive call of *Rayga, Rayga*. Looking to sea, though, I could still make out almost nothing, just a voice and a shape above the waves, biding her time until the day she might approach to ask me for my written account, my letter of love as I hoped it would then be.

There were books, too, in the rooms I rented. Piles of ancient paperbacks, spines creased white with use. I dipped into them with my bar meals, reading the way I'd always read books, as if all of these secrets in plain sight were for everyone's eyes but my own.

After eating I'd sit writing in my notebook at the end of the bar, inching the record forward while the salty shot-drinkers averted their eyes, exchanging a few soft words with one another if only to emphasize my complete irrelevance to them.

Some people shrink out of the world. The pink-eyed drinkers seemed to shrink into it. *Shadows like to meet each other*, as Opal would tell her life class. The last blackout seemed to have left a sediment inside those men that was never quite cleaned out.

A few might nod as if they knew me. Not me but my sort. Someone they'd never had any option but to tolerate. Then an apparently chance remark might bring me up short.

One jockey-sized man in a trilby hat, already seated on a high bar stool when I ordered my beer, laboriously unstrapped his wristwatch as I waited for the barrel to be changed. He reached out to lay the strap down closer to me than to his glass on the puddled zinc bar. Then he swung his upper body my way.

'Tick. Tock. Tick,' he slurred, his eyes almost level with mine, and after a beat I heard suppressed laughter behind me.

It must've been a year further on when a second man went through the same routine, with even less dexterity, though it was as if the trilby hat wearer had only just spoken.

This character paused for longer between Tick, Tock and Tick. Then he turned to the rest of the room before saying more, mainly to the table where I'd earlier been allowed to join a card game.

'He's come to wind down our clocks now!' he announced, or at least that's what I heard. 'He's the Time Being!'

It could have been a standard salute to any incomer. But in the end I mostly kept myself at arm's length, which seemed to suit everyone else. For men like those I've mentioned, this trip of mine was like an extended passing-out parade, but one they never questioned openly.

At least when I was in a public space I could keep my head down to work on my record, where increasingly I found I just had to amend, adapt or re-order words I'd written some time before.

At the best times of all I'd slip on to autopilot, and with mind elsewhere, part of a page of my thumbnail epic would appear to write itself. Perhaps the figure I could not quite see across the water was a form of muse, unlocking the words inside me, a figure with a high voice not unlike that of the mesmerizing singer I'd seen spin around.

And one evening in a bar when any sort of inspiration seemed to have deserted me, I almost didn't notice that this woman with the voice and the children had crossed my path a second time.

xlvii

There weren't many others in that immense room.

In its far corner a beatbox with fast-failing batteries was playing jazz standards. Near me on the bar stood a waterless mug holding shoots of a pink-white plant I'd seen growing wild at many roadsides, its dusty vanilla scent reminding me of a cream several of the bouquet-house women smoothed into their necks and elbows.

Intent on the page I was amending to oblivion, I'd failed to notice that my barstool was partially obstructing access to the women's washroom (though the number of women who came into these places would barely have filled one of our pinnacles).

On jerking back my upper body in mild exasperation I saw her waiting less than an arm's length away. And the eyes of a person I knew smiled back at me from the face of a stranger.

'I didn't want to distract you,' she said, dismissing my apologies as I leapt down from the stool to clear a path. 'You looked so spellbound. Braced. As if you were holding up the whole world!'

She enunciated with care, as if I might not speak her language, but as mellifluously as she sang. It was her voice that helped me make the connection. She looked so different from when she'd been marching the children along. And I used to know this. Unthinkably long ago, before the blackout even, I must have balled myself up to be hurled ahead and hit the ground at this exact spot.

From closer to, I saw lengthier softening wisps of her cropped hair curl down at her temples and on to her neck. Under a dark unbuttoned trench coat, which she'd wisely kept on in that draughty barn of a room, she wore an equally sombre-toned but very short woollen dress giving glimpses of her long, slim legs.

I took an unnecessary step further back to let her pass, taking my notebook with me off the bar. She didn't move.

'Is it going well?' she said with a nod at the book, folded open around its ring-binding at a page which, like many of the rest after so many scorings-out, now looked like Kuno's offprint.

Then she grinned, and I saw where all of Opal's swallowed smiles had gone to. Here was an even more disarming version of the girl who came to Frick in the shower, fingermarked yet innocent, and only technically more mature; something of Ute too, a woman who'd aged without growing old. I grinned back. I could've started laughing. As if from above I pictured us both in fits of uncontrollable laughter. Not sure I'd be able to speak, I tapped my pen on the book.

'Well, it doesn't get any easier,' I said.

At that she frowned, touching her lower teeth to the underside of her full top lip, her quick enquiring eyes looking all around me as if trying to get a fix from much further away.

'So is it a story?' she asked.

I should've been ready for that. Why write at all if you can't say what you've written? I couldn't even give her a title. Someone else had headed my offprint pages *Heart of Light* so I assumed something suitable would in due course be applied to this too.

'I'm not sure I'd dignify it with the word "story" – ' I began, and when she saw me cast about for a way to go on, she looked mortified.

'Oh, please forgive me! I didn't mean to pry. I'm sure real writers never like to talk about their work in progress. Maybe there aren't even words yet for what you're doing – '

No no, I insisted, there was nothing to forgive. And truly, in no sense at all could I be described as a real writer. It hadn't even been my own idea to put pen to paper –

She raised a hand. Small-fingered like a child's, no rings.

'Please, I'm really not putting you on the spot! I just find it so hard to write myself. I take all these classes, and yet – '

I cleared my throat, shook my head.

Holding both notebook and pen away from me, as if they mightn't in fact be mine, I told her that in all honesty when it came to writing, I'd never known if I was doing it properly.

'I just wait for the words, then get them down. And I'm not really doing very much now except changing what I wrote before – '

Then, still at arm's length, I flicked through the notebook's pages, to show her there was almost more blocking-out than text.

'My,' she breathed. 'You have been busy!'

Then she stepped past me to enter the washroom. I didn't move until she emerged, make-up and lipstick refreshed. With another unearthly smile she passed me again before returning to a small window alcove.

A rangy, crew-cut man much younger than herself lounged there waiting, preparing a fat cigarette. The table was strewn with pages of data as well as their wine glasses and the bottle they were sharing.

For the next half an hour they sat close together poring over these pages, while she made a few notes on a scrap of paper she took out of her large bucket-shaped shoulder bag.

She seemed to have forgotten me but it was hard to keep my eyes off them. He did the lion's share of the talking, occasionally pausing to meet her eye, then he'd ease a speculative hand along her thigh before going on. They both leaned in once to kiss.

My page on the bar swam before me as I re-played our own brief conversation. It wasn't as if I just heard it again. I saw the words paint themselves on to the bar room's dim smoky air to be re-examined.

Finally the man she was with corralled all the pages together and crammed them into a briefcase.

After standing, he swayed to the woozy music in a comically lithe way, inviting her to dance with him. She smiled as she just continued to check her bag, looking even more delicately put together now in his great strapping shadow. Yet she had spun around in mid-air with such awesome impetus that time, surely driven on by the same sweet and filthy pulse I'd seen impelling Tchure.

Then she stood. Impossibly fluently, like reversed film footage of someone sitting down. I thought of our girls rising to herald new islands; Ute up on her diving shelf: sunglasses, bare skin. And with a touch to her man's arm she came back across the floor to me.

As she approached she seemed to be struggling again to get me into focus, peppering glances all round as if seeing a kind of halo left by the coat that now hung upstairs in my room.

When she drew to a halt, my heart missed a bar's worth of beats. If this was human timber, she'd been turned on celestial lathes. Before she spoke she gave herself a moment by pausing to fasten the two large buttons on her own coat.

'You said you didn't know how to write "properly",' she began, her feline gaze swarming round me again. 'Other writers might go about it in their own way. But would that make it any more "proper"?'

When I just looked back at her, she smiled, and I sensed that under her determination to engage she was really quite shy.

'It has to be yours,' she said. 'At least in the first instance.'

I dipped my head in acknowledgement, thanking her for her interest, though even then I saw she too was acknowledging something.

'I'm sorry for what I said back there,' she went on, taking between two fingers the head of a pungent flower in the beer mug. 'About you holding up the world. It has to be that way – I know, I know.'

'And besides,' I laughed, 'I have broad shoulders!'

'You do,' she said. 'Yes, you do.'

She took her hand from the tiny flower. 'Valerian is so pretty,' she said with a sigh. 'I do love it.'

Then she swivelled on her heel as she had on the bankside, the word "love" on her lips making me catch my breath as if a bolt had been sprung somewhere just behind my breastbone.

'I'll see you around,' was the last thing she said.

xlviii

As well as running their homes and families, most bouquet-house women held down jobs. One came to me while supervising an archaeological retrieval, conserving old tombstones which turned up during repairs to a nearby port's defensive wall.

One evening after she hadn't appeared for weeks, I took a longer run to the site she'd spoken of. Unable to leave her meeting in a small pre-fabricated office, she asked a teenaged digger to take me to see some of the cleaner carved images.

In the gloaming he pointed out one spear-wielding horseman after another, arched over what looked like the same terrified naked savage. I couldn't stop seeing the latter as a child beneath a bench, and though I made a joke with the boy, I found I was holding my stomach in tight.

But one slab, crumblier, showed someone more primitive still: stocky, robed, with outstretched arms. He stood face-on in a simple flat vessel above a stylized wave that might itself have been seen as a flattened-out version of the downland heart.

Going down on one knee, I ran a fingertip over the stone's surface and felt traces of further heads behind the main, eroded disc-shaped face.

This boatman hadn't always been alone.

'So will you be staying?' the teenager surprised me by squatting down at my side and asking in a voice that hadn't yet quite broken.

When I looked his way, he peered straight back from inside his hood. Then he jerked his mineral-water bottle in the cabin's direction. 'Are you going to be staying with my mother?'

I smiled past him at the patched port wall which reared up thirty feet to a railed-off walkway. Then I stood, but the boy stayed on his haunches. We both watched his statuesque mother follow her two male colleagues out of the pre-fab and into its lean-to.

When I shook my head and told him it wasn't just up to me if I stayed, he shot me a pitying smile. A growing lad, all lips, nose and knuckles: I wished I could have waved a wand to make the rest of his body catch up quicker.

'She's wonderful,' I said of this woman I'd previously not seen by daylight. 'A wonderful person.'

He didn't respond. Instead he put an arm around the boatman tombstone. 'Have you got kids?' he said looking at the robed figure, his own scuzzy beard as convincing as Iona's felt-pen strokes when she wore my coat. I nodded, because in the sense he meant, I did.

'D'you miss them?'

My nod in reply had the force of headbutt. The twins tugged at me still the way a moon tugs at its world.

The boy's mouth flickered. He glanced at the figure's empty face, as if to present it to me again. If you don't stay, said his glance, someone else will, some indistinguishable equivalent.

I had to look away from him, back to the carved wave which may have been a heart, and I wondered why the sight of that concentration of light up on the downs had lodged in my own heart for so very long.

But the shape on the stone, keeping the robed man afloat, said something else as well. Like those shields between the corbel heads, it told me that hearts had existed before. So perhaps – when place, time and person in due course came together – there might yet be another.

'How about you?' I said to the boy. 'What are your own plans?'

He didn't appear to hear, though when I looked over, his eyes too were on where the boatman was standing.

He grunted when I said goodbye. Climbing the walkway steps I noticed the configuration of his hand, resting flat-palmed against the stone, thumb and index finger raised in the now familiar "L" gesture.

It could have been a gun shape, but both digits here seemed to be curling in. Had his hand not been empty, he might've been holding up some small object for inspection. An identity pass, a phial, a photo.

From the top of the wall I saw he hadn't moved. His mother, now standing alone with arms folded, was also looking across at him.

I'd seen something dismissive in his hand gesture, but had he just been willing me further west down this coast? Or had it not been about me at all? With his hand had he been telling me about himself, even giving me a kind of answer to my question?

Soon it will be your time, I'd have gone back to tell him if he had been ready to hear. Your world after our dark. Your laughter.

If it was mine to give, I'd have said, you could take it now.

xlix

My stopovers grew shorter as I found fewer towns, fewer bars, ever sadder little bouquet houses. (Not so much bouquets on their doors as a few herbs and leaves plaited round a small bamboo frame.)

I ran more. Setting off at dusk and jogging deep into the night. Road runs, shale tracks, cross-country, clifftop coast paths. Circuit after circuit of the few towns which still had clearly-defined surrounding walls; or, beyond them, more rustic runs around ancient quarries filled with trees and the great spoil heaps that marked the sites of long-disused mines.

There were no palisades, no protective fences. Even I could see such outposts promised little worth forcing an entry for, but someone had to count them down, and who but me would beat these bounds?

While running along the seaward side of one high wall, I heard voices and looked up.

A short procession of singing children was coming along its walkway from the opposite direction. Some looked down as they passed. The person at their head did not. It was her – the woman from the bar, stepping it out while calling back over her shoulder.

When I paused to look up, my breastbone bolt shot free again. But for all her heart-stopping looks, worn so lightly as to double their impact, she did not seize my full attention.

At the same time my ears pricked up at the song the children were chanting. The one I had heard at the retreat. It took a second or two for me to tune in to the words, but the last verse they sang before dissolving into infectious giggles came through razor sharp.

And this time, while it was actually being sung, I not only heard the lyric but I watched it scroll up into the ether as if made from individual letters of many different shapes and sizes:

Lighterman, lighterman
Show us your heart
Always together
Forever apart

Some way back I mentioned a tricky question a young boy once put to me. The boy was Muir. We'd all been in a room where his mother was playing a record, and abruptly he stalked out. I followed and found him looking disoriented. That's when he asked me what was "inside" music – as opposed to what we hear, which he called its outer skin.

Back then I could only smile, take his hand, shake my head.

But though this children's rhyme scarcely qualified as music, it made me wonder if Muir had been on to something: all human life giving rise to music's sound, from the first breath each of us takes; sound we put out that in turn can take us in. And it made my desire to reconnect with the woman conducting it as strong as the compulsion I'd felt to step inside the downland heart's inner sanctum.

By the time I ran on to the next flight of steps up, night was falling fast. I jogged back along the walkway but the procession had vanished into thin air, and without public lighting it was impossible to guess where in the town it might've been going.

At the walkway's end the inland highway rose steeply. As I began to climb, it had already grown too dark to see the overhead cables of a defunct funicular railway. Only some dimly-lit former holiday caravans were visible, standing at random angles in the laybys.

I tried the door of a small dry-stone-walled church building because I had seen kids in and around similar places before.

The pews had all been taken out, and half the interior was given over to people kneeling, not in prayer but an assembly line.

By the light of storm lanterns two women and a dozen children were making candles from boxed kits. The rest of the floor was a quilt of sleeping bags, with holdalls used for pillows.

Some of the children were still in their green blazers from the walk along the wall, sucking on packet drinks through straws. A girl who couldn't have yet been twenty, with braids coiled high on her head, came towards me at once, a powerful smell of cough linctus and damp earth gusting in front of her.

'It's only a stop-gap,' she said as if expecting a rebuke when she saw me frown at the little sea of children. 'We've just had this particular vanload a bit early.'

She ran the back of one hand across her brow, fingers streaked with tallow, then stood a little straighter in front of me. I'd thought she had come over to question my right to enter. Instead she appeared to be awaiting instruction, as ready to defer to seniority as the archaeologist's boy had been not to.

It was hard not to flinch at the fug, the unforgiving flagstones, the sense of age-old song pent up in the stonework.

I told her the house I was staying in was small but it had two empty bedrooms. I would happily move out that night to make a third if this might help a few of the kids.

The girl's expression stayed neutral.

'You'd need to take that up with the driver, sir,' she replied. 'She's only just left after bringing this new group in. She's handling accommodation now as well as transport and teaching.'

She couldn't tell me where to find this driver, but said with a grin that she could hardly imagine her heading back east. ("No one's going there now!") When I gave a brief physical description of the singer, she confirmed this was her and offered to write down her name for me.

At a lectern pushed up against the font she began to draw spidery capitals on the back of an old bus ticket. It took longer than if she'd been inscribing on sand with a stick, and I realized she was only writing at all to prove to me that she could.

While waiting, I glanced around again. In a glassed-off area stood a row of chairs, a piano, and a sink where a much older man was scrubbing plates. A red-haired boy who had just been given a treatment for headlice sat on the draining board clasping a towel around his shoulders like a miniature beaten boxer.

ALBA said the ticket the girl handed to me. No address or contact number. 'Thank you for coming in,' she said suddenly. 'We'll turn this vanload around just as quickly as we can.'

Next morning I went back. The kids were off on a nature ramble, the older man from the day before told me. He didn't expect "the driver lady" to be around again "for the foreseeable future."

When I asked where to find her, his eyes narrowed.

'Wherever they need her!' Then he asked if I'd excuse him.

'Just one thing,' I said with a smile. 'That song Alba's children were singing yesterday? What is it?'

He screwed up his face. 'Song?'

I told him I kept picking it up: a rhyme, a verse, maybe a song to march to. I *la-la-la*'d the rhythm, so he would know the song I meant, but I wanted any words to come from him.

He looked offended, as if he felt patronized.

'Nonsense,' he said, flapping both hands as if to suggest he was talking not just to me but about me too. 'Nothing but nonsense!'

Inside the porch the children's spindly self-made candles sat in a box by a wrought-metal stand. With two already burning, I put all the coins I had into the wall slot and lit a third.

On the lidded font a book of their artworks stood open at a spread given over to a collage. Magazine shots of élite athletes, grainy snaps of mothers holding newborns, a river bridge, a boatyard. A single line of cut-and-pasted print in a familiar type-size and -face ran diagonally across the foot of the right-hand page: *backing into the future on our hands and knees.*

At first glance I didn't remember I had written this while still I was part of the cohort. Then I did. And I wondered if perhaps with her teacher's hat on, Alba could've put it there.

1

With children made to sleep on flagstone floors, I no longer had the stomach to go on looking for bouquet homes. Instead I bedded down one night at a time in whatever pitiful beach shack had been left unlocked. In the last of them I hung on longer.

It wasn't fatigue that kept me from the boat morning after morning. I still ran respectable distances inland, and despite the constricted space I slept soundly. My body was telling me not just to stay, but to wait – if the reason why anyone waits is for something to start or end. As a result, the last of the bouquet-house women, Rosine, was able to run me to ground.

I returned from an evening run to find her sitting outside the shack with a picnic in a cool-bag. 'I sniffed you out!' she laughed.

We swam together first, then ate (very well), and the night was just mild enough for us to sleep out in the dunes, although subsequent nights were too cold, and Rosine brought cushions and counterpanes that made better draught excluders than upholstery.

She would come in long sleeveless denim dresses: the same style of dress in several different shades. Most mornings she managed to pick her way out of all our swaddling without disturbing me. Had I been awake when she made her own decision to take my coat for a deep clean at her place of work, I may have intervened.

The coat, it was true, was in a sad state again, thanks in part to a presumably-accidental spillage of oar-lock lubricant during one of the boat's regular phantom overnight servicings. (Rosine said she had used the term "sniffed out" advisedly.)

Two nights later she showed up with a long face.

'It fell apart,' she said. 'Disintegrated in my hands.'

Then with a roll of her eyes she stooped to unzip the cool-bag and to her own delight as much as mine produced the garment fully intact. However it had been worked on, it felt roomier, warmer. Stranger still, once the liquid solvent smell faded, its own sweeter, most historic odours all seemed to seep back.

Early one morning I pulled it on and went out to the dunes ahead of her. The new day's feeble light rose at my back, making the enormous western waters beyond the little boat look like a drab tan stew, but that was where my foreseeable future lay. It always had. A life spent chasing sunsets.

Rosine came down the shingle fingering the scarf she used as a bandanna and sometimes, on me, in more intimate ways.

'So what does the deep sea say?' she half-sang. 'Or rather, down here, the ocean.' She laced her fingers over my shoulder to peer beside me down the ragged coast. 'There's not much further to go.'

'Disappearing world,' I said, and she hooted.

'As if there's any other kind!' She paused, squeezed my shoulder, then went on. 'People always say "the end of the world as we know it" as if that's so terribly shocking. But doesn't any world we know have to end? So the next generation gets the chance to make itself a better one? All the next generations – '

Then she snuck around behind me, looped the silk scarf over my head and held it front of my eyes. Before knotting it she paused, in case I should protest, but I nodded, having guessed what might follow.

My heart beat faster as I stood statue still.

'You know where the boat's moored,' Rosine teased. 'And you know there's nothing between the boat and you. How many steps can you take towards it? Think of it like walking the plank!'

And gently she launched me forward.

'One, two, three! – ' At every number she clapped her hands, the sound ringing back off the sky. 'Four, five, six! – '

Great implausible walls reared up. Big barnacled barricades slick with seaweed. 'Seven, eight, nine! – '

At twelve I had to stop.

Next time she came, she got me to try to beat my record. So it went on. Hands raised, sometimes leading with my cheek, tensing myself before each imagined impact.

But in the darkness I "saw" something else to the west, as present as the scrolling lyrics: a grainy image of Alba the driver, swivelling from backwards to forward, backwards to forward, her electrifying performance on an endless loop above the waves.

At the end of each plank-walk the boat seemed further away than when I started, as if every blindfolded step pushed me deeper inland.

On the morning that mattered, it was even earlier than usual, still shadowy dark. I must've glanced at the boat to get my bearings before Rosine set me off. I always did. There was no reason why I wouldn't have.

Alba once more was looping her loop but soon Rosine stopped counting. I easily beat my record. Thirty-one steps. But when at last I ground to a halt and eased the scarf up on to my forehead, the boat wasn't there.

Grinning, I sat down in my coat and made myself smaller by drawing up my knees. I may even have begun to rock.

'Isn't this what you wanted?' I heard Rosine say.

Then her hand was on my shoulder. I reached up to hold it there. 'I know it's not me,' she said. 'I'm not the one.'

I shook my head, nodded, smiled. Ghostly wood shavings brushed my skin. When I shut my eyes, the driver still spun round like a ballerina in a music box, and on opening them, the westward-leading coast ahead seemed clearer.

'I've seen the way you look down there,' Rosine went on. 'If that's where you think she'll be, it's as easy on foot. There's really not much land left. Be seeing you, dear Bede.'

I sat and watched the sky fade like a bruise: blue-black into brownish-yellow then finally a filthy white. Just as the twins' existence had made Opal's milk come in, so it was in readiness for her, Alba, that I had this new sensation.

Perhaps as a parting gift, Rosine had brought me a small one-person pop-up tent in a carry bag, both sage green.

I found the coastal highway within an hour of her leaving.

It never crossed my mind to look for another boat.

li

Rosine was right. The peninsula soon tapered away, almost casually losing itself in whiter waters the way a swimmer wading out might eventually be lost to sight.

At its westernmost limit, past a decayed medieval hamlet, a tiny virtual islet clung on, reachable only at low tide across a slippery brick causeway. From above it must've looked like a teardrop about to fall.

The day I first crossed into it to mark my journey's end, I remembered Iona and Muir debating whether we in the cohort had explored or discovered the places we put in at. My heart rose here as the place discovered me.

The remains of a single, once-imposing building still stood. Whether hall, temple, palace or abbey, too little was left to be sure. Sprigs of valerian sprouted from the fractured masonry, but there were no more bouquet houses; I did go back and double-check. There were hardly any houses at all in the largely abandoned hamlet, though its handful of narrow lanes still curved and dipped with the land's contours.

Some of the dwellings, close to seriously crumbled coastal stretches, gave straight on to the sea. Their wine-coloured stone and brick all stood unrestored – barn, cottage, dovecote, brewhouse – with plenty more caravans respectfully nestling in among the fragments, many painted in rainbow stripes and paisley whorls. As with the whole peninsula, I could have been here before. Nothing I saw, smelled or heard felt entirely unsurprising.

I knew I was being watched as I walked the lanes.

Silent faces at the steamed-up windows. Kids mainly. "Urchins." Many looked at me as though they were disregarding an instruction not to stare. Possibly in response to my cheerful waves, some made the thumb-and-finger signal.

A more major road ran back inland, traffic-free, close to the promontory's sheared-off northern edge.

Some way along it, I came to a big walled-in complex of historic buildings in a much better state of repair. Two dark-suited porters stared out from a window at the foot of a monumental gatehouse, their faces lit by the same amber propane glow I'd seen in some caravans.

Beyond them, through a high pointed arch, was a courtyard (a quadrangle laid to lawn?) with a cloister at its far side. But for all the impressiveness here, the teardrop islet drew me back. My new inner sanctum.

Among the gulls and cormorants I found a ledge so thickly mossed it felt like a sofa: my final writing perch and place to wait, with a choice of relatively sheltered spots to peg down my tent in the big roofless building on the shoulder of land above it.

On another grassy slope under the pulverized perimeter wall was an old wishing well. Its water tasted fizzy. After washing there each morning, I smelled all day of blackcurrants.

For food, there were no regular shops, but back in the hamlet a tall stooping chain-smoker with a pencil moustache ran a basic store from his reclaimed cottage. Despite having a live-in step-grandson to assist him, he seemed to do little but hand-roll his cigarettes and dole out sweets to the caravan children.

I had a few banknotes from recent paid work to buy from him flat bread, chocolate, tinned fish, dried fruit. When my cash ran out Lewisohn, the old storeman, let me take what I needed if I helped him re-roof his formerly thatched cottage with sheets of corrugated iron.

One afternoon as I pulled on my coat to leave, he called me back. My notebook had dropped from the pocket. Before returning it, he flicked through its pages and laughed his soft rheumy laugh.

'That's one hell of a shopping-list you've got there, boy.'

The fingers of rock reached out to sea, the waves clawed in.

Poised above the reaching and the clawing, I tinkered away at what I had written, trying to tie up loose ends.

The rocks were like a continuation of the rubble at my back while my life lay in islands on the page. Soon now, as Kuno required, it would all be down in one place.

You don't quite belong on dry land, Muir had said. Some days when I gazed out to sea it was as if the vast waters surged in underneath me too. And I knew that she was there. No closer, no clearer, but calling to me still like a pledge of perfect music:

Rayga, Rayga –

And maybe because the washed-out light so reminded me of my other, earlier world, or because the ether here was especially porous, there were times on my perch when I almost expected to see the cohort.

Even on the calmest days I'd catch the scent of a coming wind that would flick the air inside out like a cloth pocket and just for a heartbeat show them all out there again, unwithered and undimmed: laughing, pirouetting in their overcoats, yelling obscenities. A heartbeat was all it would take. Then one of them – just one – could tie up my last loose end with a cry of "Bede, goodbye!"

On other days I'd feel impelled to set aside the notebook and look for pebbles. I made a pleasing heart-shaped arrangement of them outside the tent which I'd put up near the ruin's highest gabled wall – under a great wheel window – each stone as close as I could find to Lani's in size, shape and colour.

In the evenings then I'd run. Beating the last of the bounds.

Up at the great gatehouse of what Lewisohn had called the college, people would be visible through the arch at regular intervals. I'd re-route my runs to be there when they appeared.

Bells rang, then out they'd come into the courtyard, circling slowly in pairs: men and women, all my own age, forming a crocodile like the children who'd chanted, some in black gowns, some magenta.

Although too distant for me to make out features or words, from the way they held their heads and fluttered their hands as they spoke, they looked both confident and oblivious. They certainly never saw me jogging on the spot just beyond their walls. I'd stay until the next bell rang, before they'd all troop back inside.

So I waited. Like others in this antechamber, hunkering down, shoring up. Even the college walkers' circling looked to me like a way of waiting. The days grew so seductively still, it was as if the rocks, plants and ruins were holding their breath with us. The stillness of a course now run, all business done, however imperfectly.

I used to know this. An old world about to cede, shucking off its skin so others might wade through the flakes.

My sense of anticipation grew.

I'd last felt this way just before I saw the corbel heads. This time though, it was no set of stone heads I was about to find myself in front of, but someone else who did not quite belong on dry land, fixed in my mind forever in a sensual mid-air flip.

lii

As usual I'd reached the arch in time to watch the courtyard circlers. The bells rang out but no one showed. Nor were the porters behind their window.

I moved closer, catching my breath, then passed through.

It was, as I'd thought, a kind of quadrangle. A great half-timbered dining hall lay just inside, while directly ahead a small domed temple loomed up over the cloister. To the right stood a terrace of four-storey apartment buildings, their grey-stone chimney stacks standing like a rack of giant cricket bats.

Still no one came; nobody shouted or rushed up to muscle me out. I began to jog on the spot again, right at the edge of the walkers' gravel. Something of their energy remained, as if with all their measured movement they had built up a force field.

But when the bells rang again I was glad to turn and run back out to the road, where I heard an engine's whine.

A battered maroon minibus was approaching at speed so I stepped up onto the verge out of its way, and when it passed, the front-seat passenger gave me a cursory look. It was Alba's man from the bar. From behind I was able to make out that the driver was Alba herself.

The bus vanished down the road's next sharp dip but must have turned off, as it didn't then climb the next rise. I ran on until a ruin down below came into view at the end of a long, rutted track. I'd been aware of this place before but never given it much attention: hedged in by mature yews, bunched up close to the cliff edge, a great house so dilapidated it looked two-dimensional, little more than an ornate facade, the unshining sea showing through its mullioned windows. The old asylum, Lewisohn had called it.

On previous runs I'd seen people strolling in its wildly scenic grounds, camping out too. The house was fronted by a semi-circular, once-metalled drive, but the minibus hadn't got that far. Standing aslant on the track, it was clear to me even from up on the road that its left-side front tyre had blown.

Alba's man stood smoking beside it while she continued the descent alone on foot in her dark trench coat, carrying several bulging plastic bags in both her hands.

I ran on down the rutted track towards the bus.

Set back a short way from the house, at each end of a ravaged terrace, two better-preserved stone pavilions then came into view: twin three-storey follies with stiletto gables, at one time maybe dower houses. Alba was heading for the more westerly of the two, where I could now see small children gathered behind the barley-sugar ironwork of an upper balcony.

As I drew closer, her man was still smoking, with all the paraphernalia for changing the wheel spread at his feet – a spare with an inflated tyre, wheel chocks, jack, screwdriver. There were also more plastic bags, all stuffed with chocolate bars and cheap old mass-produced electronic hand-held games. When I saw one that Iona and Muir had used to fight over, my chest tightened.

I slowed and he smiled at me, quite winningly.

'You wouldn't know what to do here, would you?' he said.

I worked as fast as I could while keeping up a kind of conversation over my shoulder. Maybe because he had no way to make himself useful, after an initial silence he talked to me quite a lot.

The kids down in the west pavilion, he said, were scheduled to move up into the college. But now, "since both pavilions have just been requisitioned", they had to be shipped back inland temporarily to somewhere less appealing. The sweets and games were intended to soften the blow for them.

'So no one at all will be staying here soon?' I asked, merely to follow his own logic – and as soon as I spoke I realized it sounded as if I myself might be on the lookout for lodgings.

'Well,' he said, 'I believe there's someone longer-term over there.' He raised an arm in the direction of the east pavilion. 'But I'm not the best person to talk to. Not a warden or anything.'

'We're just footsoldiers,' said another voice. Alba's. 'Footsoldiers who, it emerges, can't change a wheel between us.'

liii

I think I'd already sensed her incandescent presence.

I twisted around to see her sitting on a small knoll, resting her chin on drawn-up knees, clasping her ankles above a pair of trainers as luminously white as a magpie's shoulders. On meeting my eye, she touched her lower teeth to her top lip and for a moment looked almost afraid.

'This is Reger Bede,' she quietly informed her man without looking at him. 'I'm sorry,' she said to me. 'I asked around.'

'Well so did I,' I replied, standing and wiping down my hands on my track-suit bottoms. 'I understand you're Alba.'

A smile flitted across her face. The kind of smile that Tchure might have said could fix a tyre all on its own.

'And I'm Alba's line manager,' said the other, coming forward to shake my hand. 'Thanks for your help. Thanks very much.'

As he did so, the watery sound of children's voices floated up from the west pavilion. It was the song.

'What is that they're singing?' I asked, looking from one to the other. 'I keep hearing it.'

Alba, staying seated, nodded her head at me in time to the rhythm.

'*Lighterman, lighterman?*' her man asked me back with a grin as he loaded the rest of the bags back into the bus to be driven on down. 'What does any antique rhyme mean? No one teaches it to the kids, they just seem to know it. Often they make up their own words.' He paused. 'And obviously around here there's the local connection.'

When he saw I hadn't caught his drift, he tilted his head towards the entire range of buildings below, its lengthy two-dimensional frontage, the pair of pavilions.

'"Lighterman's Reach"?' he said. 'Or at least that's what it used to be called.'

'When it was an asylum?' I asked.

'Oh, these old places, there's not much they haven't been!'

And throughout the exchange Alba went on nodding at me, the fierce look in her limpid eyes communicating that while the big man meant well, he was being far, far too prosaic. Then the song cut out, and the bus's two-way radio crackled into life.

'I'll have to get that,' said the line manager. 'Thanks again.'

I turned to Alba, now on her feet, but instead of returning at once to her driver's seat in the cab beside him, she stepped right up to me, a little colour rising in her cheeks.

'So how are you?' I asked when she didn't speak.

It wasn't just a question to pave over a space. With her I meant every syllable. I wanted to find out to the tiniest detail how, who, why and when this person was. I wanted very much to know too what it was that she herself had been trying to write.

There was recognition in the slightly withdrawn smile she gave me in reply, but maybe also an element of disbelief.

'You're here,' she said.

'Well, nearby,' I told her, prosaic in my turn.

Pointing my thumb back over my shoulder I indicated the islet.

'The close?'

She said the word to rhyme with "dose", gazing past me in the islet's direction: the gull-stained rocks, the lofty wheel window, the new spits in the air out there that could have been sea spray or rain. Her eye then seemed briefly to be caught by something further out to sea, something close to home perhaps that she hadn't been expecting and didn't yet know how to process. A shape; pure light in negative space.

'It's not going to be getting any brighter for a while,' she said. 'But you'll nearly have finished your writing?'

'Soon,' I told her. 'Very soon.'

Her line manager called out to her and she went up on tiptoe to kiss the corner of my mouth.

'Soon,' she repeated.

There was music in the way she walked smartly back to the bus, gunned it up then careered on down the track. I'd heard it too when she'd been sitting stock still on the knoll.

Soon. And not just for her, and not just for me.

liv

Within two days, the great house had been ringed by orange incident tape and work teams were making internal alterations on the pavilion that had housed Alba's children.

On each of my runs down the track it seemed that more people, of all ages, had congregated in the grounds, often with their dogs, reclining on the grass in curved rows which fanned back from the other, eastern, pavilion as if this was an open-air stage from which a show might eventually be mounted. Meanwhile they picnicked, played ball sports, or gingerly negotiated the steps hewn out of the cliff-face down to a long wharf.

From time to time on O I'd seen similar trancelike crowds gathering for an eclipse or new year. But there they'd been well-heeled, self-assured. These freer spirits looked as if they had nowhere else to be. Many of the children went shoeless.

Whenever I ran through, some of the kids broke away from their families to the trackside. They'd clap and cheer me on.

Sometimes a small group struck up the "antique" rhyme, but after the first line or two their elders would call over to make them stop.

I'd also see the way these relatives eyed me, and their expressions were familiar. *If someone has to do this* – 'He's the human dynamo!' one young woman in a ragged kaftan cried, then blushed ferociously when I gave her the thumbs-up.

There was no more to see at the college.

A blackened, bolted door closed off the gatehouse arch. No lights glowed behind the glass, no one looked out. But from the track down to the pavilions its high rear wall stood in full view, and twice I noticed ungowned individuals using a more modest wicket gate set into it.

The whole building's orientation seemed to be altering. Where once it had looked out on to the road, and from there back inland, its attention had now been switched to the sea.

Old Lewisohn's step-grandson, a louring late teen who snickered into his sweat-top hood whenever he saw me, had taken himself off. Without him around, the caravan kids came in and took what they wanted. They threw pebbles at the new iron roof. Soon Lewisohn stopped flinching at every crack and rattle.

'Nothing's new,' he said to me during one of the raids, pushing a hand back through his tough-looking hair. 'We used to have youth on our side, now it comes at us head on!'

He blew two perfect smoke-rings, then gave his soft smile.

He said his boy had gone to paint walls for "decent money" in the emergency refurbishment. 'And he'll have a bit more to paint once they've winkled our friend out of the east wing!'

'Our friend?'

'I use the term elastically,' he conceded. 'But friends are what you need, and for some while now we've appeared to need him.'

I got the feeling this person may once have been an "owner" like Opal back on O, someone whose estate had gradually shrunk to no more than the carpet he sat propped up on, and soon even this would be whipped out from under him.

'They should've moved him on when his wife passed,' said Lewisohn. 'It may be too late to get him out in one piece. He's not a well man. Not well at all. Then again, which of us is?'

In the deeper watches of the night I'd dream that my rocky tear-drop cried itself away from the mainland. On its back I would drift out to meet the figure who never quite came closer. And they would be there too. My people in the boats. Stone-faced now, waiting to say goodbye, and so send me further on.

Good things, quietly underpinned these dreams.

All those spirited women I'd had the good fortune to know since leaving O (and arguably even Lani and Opal before that time) had surely been sounding me out. Putting me like a shell to their ears, then passing me on down the line, from station to station.

While adding the finishing touches to my "shopping-list" – this untitled story that mightn't be a story, the word-sheet to my life-song – I'd study the horizon as more light drained from each day. A lid was coming down, achieving the new blackout by degrees. With Alba and her children I had caught a sense of some wholly new vibration. Now silence wrapped it round, but still it was there, alive at the core.

Ever since the cohort left me stranded, my own spiral groove had been bringing me here, guiding me through to the centre of the disc, though what counts is the larger, richer, living sound that the disc can touch off. And sometimes, if you listen before lifting the needle on its tone-arm, a recorded surprise may be lurking in the runout.

lv

I ran now only by day. At night it was too hard to navigate the milling crowds, most of them finally drifting across to the house once known as Lighterman's Reach.

There seemed to be just enough of everything. Enough light, enough warmth. Enough time – I didn't doubt – for everyone to do what still remained to be done.

As I ran past the college, an ambulance with a flashing blue light gave me a wide berth. In such a drowsily mellow atmosphere the idea of an emergency seemed quite alien.

I didn't know where the vehicle had been despatched from, nor where it would be heading once its patient was on board, but its arrival in the mansion's grounds could not have been better timed to coincide with my own.

A panelled fence had replaced the work team's orange tape, and from the lack of activity around the west pavilion it appeared that the refurb on that side was complete.

The ambulance had swung around to park some distance short of the drive in front of the east pavilion, its back doors opened in readiness, a steel ramp running down to the grass.

The assembled people seemed to be forming a loose kind of community. Not a festival crowd exactly. I sensed nothing like elation. The mood was elegiac, rather; this had to be an ending but I saw a promising neutrality in the way they all angled themselves towards one another, giving every impression that they were preparing to say goodbye in good order.

I still had to pick my way through some of them, since in many places they'd spilled on to the track. Strollers, picnickers, dog-walkers, campers, children playing tag.

Just one knot of cross-legged teenagers made the 'L' gesture at me. Coolly casual, looking away, finger and thumb so close together in each case that they could've been pinching invisible spliffs. I noticed Lewisohn's step-grandson among them.

The last time I'd seen Lewisohn he'd offered me the young man's room. 'You don't think he's coming back?' I asked.

Lewisohn laughed, coughed. 'They don't, do they? They can't.' Behind his counter he waved his hand in a dismissive arc. 'They're looking past all this now, not that they'd ever admit it. He'll move on soon. Just up and leave!'

'Some people moved on from me like that once,' I told him before I could check myself.

He looked into my eyes as if to say he already knew.

'But did you need to be left behind? For what came later? And would you have stayed of your own accord?' He quickly raised a hand. 'Please don't go to the trouble of telling me. All that matters now is now!'

I turned down his offer of the room. I'd taken enough. From the start of my journey to its end I had been catered for so kindly. Alba was wrong: it was the world that'd held me on its shoulders.

'Or if you ever want a hot bath,' Lewisohn went on, pointing through his inner doorway. 'Just go ahead.'

I was running on to less crowded ground, aiming for the coast path at the rear of the mansion, when the chanting welled up.

It seemed to come from the sea, or even some underground chamber, rather than from the kids who were now some distance behind me. But it was to them that I turned.

No one was within fifty paces. And there wasn't the slightest breeze. But the little nonsense song swirled around me as powerfully as the anthems Opal had played on my first visit to the lighthouse then never again, its words as clear as day:

> *Lighterman, lighterman*
> *Show us your heart*
> *Always together*
> *Forever apart*

Only that. Over and over, louder then softer then louder again.

Shutting my eyes, I was back beneath the bench, the sweet smell of shavings filling so much more than just my nose.

In all the years I'd been without them too, I had never felt so close to my cohort. But when I looked, though the song rang on, no one in the crowd appeared to be singing.

Instead there had been a mass gravitation, like a smudge of evening starlings, in the direction of the east pavilion. And I could just make out three yellow-jacketed paramedics hefting someone in a wheelchair down its front flight of steps.

I had to retrace my route, the song drawing me back like a rope coiled round my waist while simultaneously carving out a channel through the throng ahead of me.

It was the back of his head I saw first. Just a glimpse before the female paramedic started wheeling him towards the ambulance. The same head I'd seen on returning to our block all those light years before. Another evening, another run. A man so much younger then, stripped to the waist, about to throw himself into his foul-mouthed war-dance.

I had made false projections before: misidentifying from behind a person who'd been out of my life for so much longer than ever they'd been in it – my life if not my thoughts or my heart, which now beat so loudly that it silenced the song.

But already I knew this was no misidentification.

At the ramp the two male health workers took over, positioning themselves fore and aft of the wheelchair, then carefully turning it to face me prior to easing it up into the ambulance.

The patient's upper body sagged sideways with the motion, so that just before he could be straightened he was able to peer around the stooped paramedic and watch me come to a dead stop in front of him.

His mouth took a long time to open, but his voice, when it came, had barely aged.

'Dear boy!'

I sank to my knees. I hadn't planned to, but at least now my eyes and his were on a level.

I reached out, and on the rug stretched across his bloated knees I closed my hands over both of his, horribly swollen too yet sorrowfully clawlike. The whole of him seemed inflated, even his nose, his lips, the pits which had always scarred his skin and now made a moonscape of his face. Oh, Tchure. Tchure.

They'd said maybe we were divine, and if ever there was a storm god in the making it was this beloved brother of mine. I might have imagined Tchure going up finally in his own flame, but never the prospect that faced me now.

'So this is us!'

He said it brightly. Infinitely too brightly. His eyes with nothing behind them fixed on mine.

In the hush around us people were taking photos. I caught the detonations at the edges of my vision.

The three paramedics hovered, half-looking away, giving us space. Waiting perhaps for a signal from Tchure to proceed – if he was any longer able to make that kind of call.

I lowered my head and let it rest on our hands.

Fruit, steeped in spirits. Wood shavings, fruit cake.

I think Tchure may have laughed.

I felt him try to stir one hand. When I drew back just far enough to look up into his bulging pallid face, he winched the hand with visible effort towards my cheek.

Between his thumb and index finger he made a hopeless pass at plucking at my great mess of a beard, the skin on his own sad face supporting nothing more than a few rogue wisps.

'Is all this,' he said as briskly as before, 'strictly necessary?'

He laughed, moving no part of himself save his lower jaw.

'No sharp objects!' he barked, then he laughed even harder.

I saw the female paramedic put a hand across her mouth.

Giggles bubbled up on every side in the watching crowd. More cameras sparked against the dying light. Guffaws then.

Not malicious laughter, I knew that. None of this was meant to hurt or humiliate. I had to smile too, if only to keep at bay a welter of so many conflicting emotions.

First I smiled at Tchure, then at those standing nearest, some with babies in slings, others with kids on their shoulders.

And out of nowhere poor Tchure stirred himself to give me what I needed.

Grabbing a fistful of my beard, he pulled me so close I smelled aniseed and turnips on his breath. 'You always had too much for us!' he hissed into my eye. 'Bede's the man! But now you've served your time. Goodbye, dear boy. Goodbye, goodbye!'

Then releasing me, he turned his attention to everyone else.

'It's time!' he declared, for all the world as if he'd been wheeled here on this small throne specifically to deliver an edict to his subjects. 'This is the time!' he hollered.

The paramedics moved fast, hauling him up the ramp and slamming him inside almost before I got back on my feet.

Moments later the ambulance moved off, and instinctively I continued my run in its slipstream, with warm applause now rippling in from both sides. I hadn't yet done with Lighterman's Reach, and certainly not with Alba. But now that my decks had been cleared, a few last things needed to be put in order.

I ran to the top of the track at its junction with the road, and when the vehicle turned to gather speed in an inland direction, I made again for the sea.

lvi

I hardly left my tent for a week, with each day both starting and ending darker than the last. This was not the depletion I had known when my whole cohort left – this wasn't depletion at all – nor had it been caused just by Tchure. What I felt at first was great weightlessness, as if like the tent I needed pegging down in place.

Through the fine new rains I lay watching my rocky perch peter out into the ocean, step by blindfolded step. Then foraging nearby I found some small stones to form the figure "14" inside the pebble heart, the number on all of Tchure's lockers.

It's time! rang in my ears. *This is the time!*

The single word *Soon* sounded too. Back in the grounds, facing Tchure in his chair, I had grasped what set Alba apart. In all the years since my people moved on, she alone could have been one of us: the wearer of a numbered coat, a string to bring new resonance to our own living instrument: entrancing me just as the twins had entranced me, by proving there could still be wonders.

From that point, whenever I pictured her marching at the head of a column of kids, she moved to the pulse of the heart of light, and to me this was a new kind of love.

But I hadn't entered Alba's air space, nor she mine. This had to be somewhere new for us both – a place, once found, that could surely not be lost.

On running out of food, I went back to Lewisohn and took him up on his offer of a bath.

On the sink-mirror shelf he'd put out a cut-throat razor. New blades in little rice-paper envelopes. In ten minutes I lost the beard of decades that Tchure had rightly questioned, the hairs I scoured out of the plughole mostly whiter now than grey.

Each time I turned full-on to the mirror, another pair of eyes – older and younger than my own – came swinging towards me out of their own unrelievable gloom. A road at night: two bikes, one light. *My parents had to let me go.* With just the moustache I could perhaps have passed for Lewisohn's son.

Then I shaved myself fully clean. And the blade was still sharp enough for me to shear away the greater part of my head hair too.

'Welcome back,' said Lewisohn when he saw the new old me.

He asked me to help him fix back into place a makeshift ceiling support that had begun to buckle towards the rear of his home. Then I was glad to accept his invitation to stay for dinner, where we drank far more of his home-brewed hooch than we ate food.

Throughout the evening waves of unthreatening noise surged overhead. Baying voices, chanting and cheers; there may have been airy music threaded through it. The number of people in the great house's grounds could only have swollen again.

Lewisohn shrugged when I asked why they all came.

'They probably wouldn't be able to explain it themselves,' he said, locating a thread of tobacco on his tongue and picking it off. 'You go with it, though, don't you? Reasons can come later.'

I nodded, recalling the morning I'd woken up on O with Tchure and all the others gone. I'd been able to make no sense of it at the time, but soon in that place I would be with the twins.

Having rolled cigarettes for us both, Lewisohn splashed out the last of the liquor. 'The mystery continues,' he said, raising his glass and moving it from side to side to inspect its contents. 'Until we die we're being born. But we each make our own microscopic difference. Missing even the humblest instrument, the orchestra falls apart. It all adds up, it has to, probably to more than we ever shall know!'

He looked at me pointedly through the liquid. Through it I looked back and saw other swirling worlds, fused now in a heart of light. Light veneered by sound: the sound of just one sphere.

'To you and all who sail in you!' was Lewisohn's final toast.

'To us,' I tried to counter.

But he wasn't having that.

'You,' he insisted. 'It is you.'

There was a moment after I said goodnight to him – already staggering a little, and made more dizzy by the clouds of dope smoke wafting over – when I toyed with heading not towards my place of vigil but in the opposite direction, to check on the seaboard party which out of doors sounded so much louder.

It really was only a moment.

Then flicking up the collar of my coat against the chill, I returned to the spot I had made my final station. The reason for that was no mystery at all. Out on the rocks was where she would find my letter of love, with me curled up around it.

5

lvii

Gently she shook me awake, her hand reaching in for my shoulder, her exquisite voice in my head.

Rayga, Rayga – Calling it, cooing it.

The figure from across the sea.

A woman. The woman.

'Come now,' she was saying, tremulous with excitement. The woman who was Alba. 'Bring your things and come – '

I propped myself up on my elbow in the tent. She was beckoning me, her face dark and small against an umber sky.

She stood back to let me shamble out, still wearing my coat, and I watched her eyes widen as she saw me shaven and shorn, which brought me so much closer to the air.

'You don't need your tent!' she said when I started to dismantle it. But I gathered up the rest, leaving just my little heart shape made of pebbles. When she led me away to cross the causeway, it was to make for a small grey van.

I still hadn't fully woken, and not just from my sleep of the night before. With a sweep of her arm she cleared some digital disc cases off the passenger seat.

'It's fine,' she assured me breathlessly, smiling as she tried to make the engine bite. It took her a while. The discs weren't hers but her manager's, she said, nodding to suggest they were maybe not to her own taste. She'd been meaning to get them back to him, she went on once we set off, her hand brushing mine on changing gear. Something she had now come out of.

The van wasn't easy to manoeuvre. No power steering, windscreen wipers that never quite dispersed the more stubborn drizzle. In the narrow curving lanes she gave all her concentration to avoiding the sides of the caravans; avoiding people too as they dreamily straggled down from the college approach road, on to which with a heartfelt gasp of relief she finally swung the vehicle.

'This is all on account of the big party last night,' she said, shooting glances my way. 'The welcome party? Though it turns out they're not actually staying, just passing through to let the last few join up. And after all that preparation!'

Another glance.

'I thought you'd be there. At the party? I looked for you.'

I smiled at her, waiting, feeling much as I did on the morning I travelled back to O after the storm. That same oyster light of a not-quite-breaking day. The light we'd all known for so long before we went up on to the downs.

Beyond the college she slowed, then took the descending track after letting a queue of cars from below make their exit first.

The grass on the slope was thick with streamers, bottles, paper cups, abandoned sleeping bags, barbecue stands.

Still I waited, half-turned to her in my seat.

She must have just come from this party herself. Her narrow blue velvet trousers and ankle boots. The cream crew-necked pullover she kept hitching up over her bare shoulder. Tucked behind her ear she wore a poppy-like flower Lani once said that she liked. It may have been called a hibiscus.

She knew I was looking and gave me a smile.

'I didn't know it'd be like this!' Lightly she laughed. 'Any of it. I just didn't want you to miss them, you know? Then I can show you something else. I wouldn't want to offend you. But if you actually get to see it, you might then think differently about it – '

She left the track and pulled up with a jolt that sent the disc cases skittering. Four other vehicles of roughly the same size were parked nearby, their middle-aged male drivers standing together to share a steaming drink from a flask. Open-mouthed children lay fast asleep on the seats inside, their faces pressed to the windows.

'We'll have to walk the rest,' said Alba, opening her door. 'You can leave your things here.'

She didn't seem to have a coat. Already I'd registered that she wasn't dressed to be outside, but when I offered her my own garment she smiled as if I'd made a joke and struck out ahead.

The new fence was still quite distant. None of the remaining cars or vans had parked any closer, nor did the party debris reach this far. We walked on side by side down the track, Alba in her two-inch heels adroitly picking a way across the ruts.

From the moment I left the van I was counting each step in my head. I'd not been this close to the east pavilion before. It reared up high above the fence.

Pushing my hands deeper into my coat pockets, I felt for the edge of my notebook, my biros. Alba smiled. Happy. She wanted me to be happy, I knew she did. And a world hadn't yet been formed where I would not have wanted the same for her.

On step number fifty the ether altered. My heart folded out and filled my chest. People were moving behind the pavilions' frosted windows. Both pavilions. Some were on the balconies.

Young people, younger than I ever remembered being, all of them dressed for travel.

'They were here?' I sounded so far away, my voice all but breaking. 'In the pavilions – boys in one, girls in the other?'

Alba nodded and gave her light tuneful laugh.

'Well, they'd probably prefer you to call them young men and young women!'

Losing count, I strode on faster. Walking in a state of worship. In front of us, a pair of makeshift gates had been pegged back to form an exit through the fence at the rear, near to the edge of the cliff where steps then led down to the wharf.

Alba had to trot to keep up.

'Hey!' she laughed. 'We're in good time!'

lviii

They streamed out of the compound and made straight for the cliff steps. A host of streaky youngsters. No faces, only hoods pulled up against the mist and drizzle. Coded whispers, earphone wires, arm brushing arm as they passed through the gateway and followed one another down the steps.

Some of the girls carried old-fashioned books while others held laptops, tablets, or consulted bulky cell-phones. The skies ahead of them were impossibly wide. No horizon.

I felt Alba's hand on my arm, but she wasn't aiming to stop me from seeing the pinnaces below being dragged into deeper water, several already holding their complement, with many smaller children in place to see them off. She was just looking out for me, drawing me back from the edge of the cliff.

Her hold on me grew firmer, and still looking down I placed my hand over hers. I heard a small, choked cry. It came from me, so far was I past words. But through our continuing contact, even as we stood rooted we were moving closer to the new heart of light.

These are my people! I told Alba with my eyes. And her own eyes said something back. Something I was too euphoric in that moment to register, but soon now I would.

They'd all partied hard, some actually having to help others along. Then up loomed the first face I knew, angled my way from a band of loose-limbed boys tripping past, one prayer among the many.

The archaeologist's son: lips, nose, scuzzy beard. Looking but not seeing. Not knowing me since he no longer needed to.

I put out a hand – my arm hanging loose to prove I presented no threat – and brushed his kagoul sleeve with my fingertips. Barely breaking step, he looked down, then back at my face. Forgotten, all forgotten.

Still Alba held my arm, reinforcing with her grip what I still hadn't fathomed she had told me with her eyes. Closing my hand tighter over hers, our fingers entwined.

Others in the marchpast looked my way. Self-conscious girls, uncertain boys, most of them hooded, so many of their faces half-familiar from my travels since leaving O – had all these really come in my wake? – some with heart shapes marked in biro by their eyes. My children, all my children.

Lewisohn's step-grandson came. His head alone uncovered, black hair now buzz-cut close to his skull; the swagger of a newly-minted ringleader, accepting an opened can of beer from the boy at his side. He watched me hard as he passed, all but brandishing his can. My hand pawed thin air. He'd wiped me completely. Me, us, the ground we stood on, the fading shapes of everything they had to leave behind as we sent them on ahead.

These were, and were not, my people.

Hoods not coats. A new cohort, new and full of echoes, still deep inside its own darkness, still on the outward passage before the laughter could start, seeing only in.

Had I thought they might listen, I'd have blessed them. I'd have told them not to laugh too soon. And knowing that they couldn't listen, and shouldn't, filled me with such pride and hope.

'They're beautiful,' Alba murmured. 'So beautiful – '

There weren't many of them left, a straggle of slower-moving back markers. A well-built young man left the compound alone, shunting a cell-phone into his pocket. He veered in my direction, his face more than half-obscured by his hood but I knew him.

I knew him.

I took a step his way, Alba's hold on me loosening.

He was dawdling, taking one step marginally nearer to me, then one the same distance away, clearly having seen me from inside the fence and in two minds about what to do next.

Two indistinct others came on behind.

A girl with both hands resting on a small but definite distension of her stomach, and a young male partner with his arm draped just as protectively around her.

The boy on his own stood taller than me now.

Inside the hood I saw his eyes, his frown. I used to know this. I used to know him and love him and I always would. But still he might've drifted past, actively unseeing, had I not reached out to seize his wrist with my free left hand, then thrown up my arm around his sturdy shoulders and drawn him toward me.

'Boy – ' I gasped into his neck. Through the incense, male sweat and nicotine I thought I still smelled baby lotion. 'My boy – '

He tensed but not to resist. I felt him fold me in.

Then a new hand came between us, prising us slightly apart. Not Alba's hand. Still she was standing to my right, her hold on me unrelinquished. It was the girl who'd left her young man standing. A pair of almond eyes gleamed up into my own. Her too! My love doubled.

Inching her twin brother aside, she slid inside our embrace.

Alba tried to extricate herself but I wouldn't let her go. For as long as this might last, she belonged with us, her breath as a part of our chorus, these children hers as much as mine.

The chorus swelled, and then we went deeper.

A new heart of light had been formed.

A light not from above but from us: our light inside the skin of sound. This was what had to add up. All the life in us, the love in us, taking us beyond ourselves to a place not there before; the actual whole of music is when we become it.

And even as I quaked with exaltation, I felt a hand probe the pocket of my coat.

Then Muir and Iona were gone.

When I blinked the dampness from my eyes, they both were on the steps. By the time they completed their descent they may have forgotten I'd been there, distilled me down to a single inscrutable image, their own pair of legs at a woodworker's bench.

But they'd be back, after the ocean, after all the new and endless chains of islands, back from the far side of whatever lay ahead. These people who would have no past, and so had the chance to surpass not just us but themselves.

Alba leaned into me as we watched them strike out through the tranquil waters, the silence between us as natural as it was freighted.

These are my people! I'd tried to say just by looking at her. Until our embrace I had failed to decipher the look she'd given me back, but our moment of convergence brought it home.

We're your people, was what it said. I am. It's me. It is me.

When I looked I saw her eyes had filled with tears.

'Oh I'm so sorry,' she said shaking her head. 'Mine, too, have just gone. That's all. As I always knew they'd have to – '

I turned her in to me and she held me as fast as I held her.

'Ours,' I said. 'They're all ours now.'

With the boats still in sight, the smaller children started scrambling up from the water's edge. Quietly confident children, some inspecting the heart shapes painted on one another's temples. A girl measured with her thumb and index finger one boy's, and on taking away her hand they both gasped at its size.

Alba drew back a short way. She touched my face, dried her eyes, then went across to where they had gathered.

She said something that made them laugh, and chatted for a short while longer before sending them over to the other drivers who were still standing near her van. She would never not be there for the children. I looked at her and loved her. The entire cubic content of her.

When she walked back towards me, the dark air she passed through flowed more slowly, as if in appreciation. I stood straighter, feeling lighter. There was new weight in my pocket, though.

I reached in and as soon as my fingers closed around it, I had no need to take it out to see what it was. Lani's pebble, returned by Iona.

Then Alba was in front of me, smiling but also shivering, shuddering. It really was too cold. I pulled off my coat to throw around her shoulders, and this time she made no protest.

lix

Then Alba showed me why else we had come. To see a room inside the east pavilion. ("The one where the young women stayed, if it's all the same to you!") A place where, she very tentatively suggested, I might like to continue with my writing.

Still morning had not properly broken. It wasn't going to now, and there was no telling how long it would be before the sun shafted through again. Inside the pavilion it was night-time dark, as dark as it always was inside our blocks at ground-floor level. In the absence of any power, tea lights stood burning in small saucers on many of the surfaces.

Before climbing the staircase after Alba, who bunched up my coat in both her hands like a ball gown, I caught sight of the dressing room and showers. Windows low and frosted, many of the grey metal lockers with their doors ajar. We didn't climb as far as the third storey, the sleeping quarters. I wasn't going to have to worry about dorms any more.

It still smelled of fresh paint from the refurb. Magnolia in the stairwell, gardenia on the walls of the fairly disorderly recreation room, which was more or less the same size as the dressing room and shower area below. A couple of doors led off up here.

We'd often seen similar doors, always locked. Glorified cupboards, we used to assume. Storage spots for cleaning equipment, linen, replacement towels.

One of the doors was open.

Alba pushed it further back, then after dropping a droll little curtsy she stood aside and gestured for me to go in.

'If you felt you could work here,' she said from the doorway, 'I've been given clearance for you to use it, at least until they requisition the building again, and that won't be any time soon.'

'But the children – ' I began, and had to stop and start again because my voice had turned to sandpaper. 'Won't you want to move your kids back in?'

'They were in the other pavilion,' she reminded me. 'But yes, they'll soon return there. A last few lots of children will be coming to this building too. Kids and their carers – who'll always be able to make use of an extra pair of hands, should you feel like taking a break from your labours!'

In the steady light from the faintly fragrant candles dotted around the room, her eyes flashed.

'We have the capacity to generate enough power when we need it. And now that the curtain's coming down, I'll be spending more time here myself – '

I sized up the room. It hadn't been redecorated with the rest of the block and looked like a museum mock-up, somebody's living quarters from thirty, forty years before. Maybe once it had been a kind of caretaker's lodging. Maybe it had been Tchure's.

And I surely used to know this.

A bed that would take two people at a pinch, a fireplace with white ash mounded in its grate, two armchairs, an imitation-antique roll-top bureau with a matching straight-backed seat; and on a low chest sat a portable record player, its latched lid raised, with the artwork on the sleeves of some of the vinyl albums fanned out next to it already striking distant chords.

French doors, ajar, gave on to a dainty little ironwork balcony, then the sea.

I went right up to them to look out and, when I narrowed my eyes, almost beyond the sea there were tiny flecks which may or may not have been the boats of the newest cohort.

'The room next door is a kitchen,' said Alba. 'There's no shortage of provisions – the last people through barely touched them! The washing and laundry facilities are down on the first floor – '

As I turned back to face her, she stopped speaking.

Then she shook her head at the way in which the two of us had been guided so unerringly along our separate paths to the threshold of the next new night.

'Oh, and there's this,' she said, crossing to the bureau to my left.

The key in its lock took a moment's manipulation before it would turn at the required angle. Then with the flourish of a magician's assistant she rolled up the slatted lid to reveal on the inlaid writing surface a small red typewriter and a stack of blank paper.

'It's just that I thought – ' she began, dipping a hand into the pocket of my coat, and although she'd presumably intended to take out my notebook, she produced instead the pebble.

She admired it in her palm before setting it down to one side of the typewriter then reached in the pocket again to remove my book, which carefully she placed on its other side.

'I wondered if it might perhaps be a tiny bit easier for all your future readers, if you were to – ?'

And in making a mime of typing with both hands, I saw her conducting an orchestra, and maybe even heard its swell.

The typewriter could have been a Voormann Park exhibit, possibly a child's model, its bright red paint tarnished here and there.

This, then, was how it would be.

I'd be seated at this bureau consecrated by the presence of Lani's pebble, my ring-bound love letter to Alba folded back for transcribing, while elsewhere in the building I'd hear children singing their serenades, not for me any more but for cohorts still to come, hardwired for hope, in the darkness that had to keep falling so that they could all then shine; children whose everyday welfare would become my own prime concern too, since my "labours" at the bureau could not go on indefinitely.

'If you're not a typist already,' Alba was saying, 'there's really nothing to it. I taught myself in just an afternoon! But if – '

I laughed. 'No ifs. I see no ifs here at all.'

I thanked her profusely – and it's hard to imagine a person who looked more pleased or relieved than Alba did then. This shy lucid beauty who stood swamped in my coat and called herself a footsoldier, as if there are any other ranks.

'You're really most welcome,' she said quietly, touching a fingertip to my chest as though to check for a specific kind of warmth and seeming, miraculously, to find it. 'Ours,' she told me, repeating what I'd said when we stood out on the cliff. 'Ours now. All of it.'

Through fresh tears she smiled.

'And I'd be honoured,' she made herself go on, 'to be the first person to read your typed-up story. Even if you don't actually dignify it with the word "story" – '

At that point I turned back to the French doors, aware that if I continued to look at her, this might all become too much.

lx

Alba said more. I knew what she was saying but her words were muffled, baffled, by all the sounds I must've stored inside myself while waiting for this moment, tiny in themselves but powerful in concert, a thousand old houses settling in the night.

All that mattered now was now.

I'd always been beguiled by time. This woman took time away. Of course I had written a story. One of the oldest. The story of a man serially entranced, of a life not so much lived as affirmed with his every breath and step since the last blackout.

A story I'd been put in and was on the point of leaving.

The sky above the sea had darkened fast. A single small pale drizzly area now stood out, a perfect match in shape for the elusive form we had glimpsed so long before on the downs – an aperture just large enough for a celestial hand to reach through, lift the needle from the record, steer the tone-arm back to its rest and bring the turntable to a halt.

I heard different music. Soft and new but full of echoes. Music for more than the ear. Music that, with Alba, I could be.

I swung around, afraid she'd be gone, that all I'd ever done was dream her. But there she stood, as real as me.

She'd closed the door, hung my coat from its peg, taken all the little flickering candles from the shelves and mantelpiece and arranged them on the floor between us to recreate the shape I had seen in the sky. Our music had become the room.

Smiling in the way that only she could, Alba held out both arms to me. Then together we stepped inside the heart of light.